W9-CXN-338

William
and the
Witch's Riddle

Also by Shutta Crum

Thomas and the Dragon Queen

WILLIAM
and the
WITCH'S RIDDLE

by **Shutta Crum**
illustrations by **Lee Wildish**

Alfred A. Knopf   New York

For Judi, Brandon, and Olivia—dragon lovers!
—S.C.

Text copyright © 2016 by Shutta Crum
Jacket art and interior illustrations copyright © 2016 by Lee Wildish

All rights reserved. Published in the United States by Alfred A. Knopf, an imprint of Random House Children's Books, a division of Penguin Random House LLC, New York.

Knopf, Borzoi Books, and the colophon are registered trademarks of Penguin Random House LLC.

Visit us on the Web! randomhousekids.com

Educators and librarians, for a variety of teaching tools, visit us at RHTeachersLibrarians.com

Library of Congress Cataloging-in-Publication Data
Names: Crum, Shutta, author. | Wildish, Lee, illustrator
Title: William and the witch's riddle / by Shutta Crum ; illustrations by Lee Wildish.
Description: First Edition. | New York : Alfred A. Knopf, [2016] | Summary: William must solve a witch's riddle in order to save his family and end a centuries-long curse.
Identifiers: LCCN 2015033294 | ISBN 978-1-101-93269-8 (trade) |
ISBN 978-1-101-93270-4 (lib. bdg.) | ISBN 978-1-101-93271-1 (ebook)
Subjects: | CYAC: Riddles—Fiction. | Witches—Fiction. | Blessing and cursing—Fiction. | BISAC: JUVENILE FICTION / Action & Adventure / General. | JUVENILE FICTION / Family / Siblings. | JUVENILE FICTION / Legends, Myths, Fables / Other.
Classification: LCC PZ7.C888288 Wi 2016 | DCC [E]—dc23

The text of this book is set in 14-point Galena.

Printed in the United States of America
September 2016
10 9 8 7 6 5 4 3 2 1

First Edition

Whiter than snow is love's light atremble.
Thirteen for Morga—scooped in a thimble.

Redder than blood are flames that will brand.
Thirteen for Morga—clutched in bare hand.

Blacker than night is death's icy kindle.
Thirteen for Morga—fixed on a spindle.

A thimble of love.
A handful of flame.
A spindle of death.
And I'll go whence I came.

BOOK I

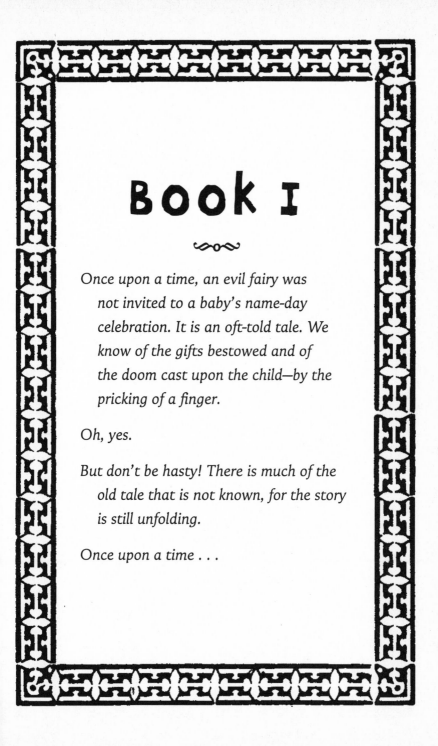

Once upon a time, an evil fairy was
   not invited to a baby's name-day
   celebration. It is an oft-told tale. We
   know of the gifts bestowed and of
   the doom cast upon the child—by the
   pricking of a finger.

Oh, yes.

But don't be hasty! There is much of the
   old tale that is not known, for the story
   is still unfolding.

Once upon a time . . .

chapter 1

William held two shrunken turnips. Turnips and apples—that was all the food they had. He chewed his lip.

"When's Da coming home?" Pinch asked once more.

And again William answered, "Soon." Their father made the trek down the mountain to the village regularly and was usually home in a couple of days. Never had he been gone this long.

They could wait another day. But if Da did not come, they would have to leave. They'd be completely out of food. William had been down Crag Angorm before—as far as the high pastures to help with the goats—but not without his father, not in winter, and not with his little brother, Pinch.

Pinch put his thumb in his mouth.

"Don't suck your thumb! You've got almost five summers."

"I'm hungry." Pinch stuck his lip out.

"Tonight you can have an extra-big helping. I'm not . . . not that hungry."

"You're not?" Pinch looked up. "Can you tell me a story about Mama tonight?"

Stories about their ma were Pinch's favorites. But they reminded William of how alone they were. Their mother had gone down the mountain last spring and never returned. Since then, Da often went in search of her. And now, at the tail end of winter, he had not come home. William said, "I'll tell you one if you don't pester me."

Pinch ran in circles yelling, "Pesk! Pesk! Pesker!"

William laughed. "It's *pest*," he corrected his brother.

They were both feeling restless. Snow had pummeled **their little house, tucked up at the peak of the crag, for** days. Still, if Da did not return tomorrow . . . they would have to leave their snug home and go down the mountain to find him.

William dreamed of his mother. In his dream her laughter was quick and light like the tinkling of goat bells. He tried to hold her there. But she always faded—down the path to the valley.

William moaned. He woke with his heart clacking against his rib cage. It was colder than it should be. One of the shutters had blown open.

He wrapped a coverlet around himself and went to close it. He peeked out. Against the white of snow-covered boulders, something was moving. Da? Then a cloud passed, and in the moonlight he saw that the figure didn't move the way Da did.

But who would be up here in the middle of the night? And in winter? Only twice, in the summertime, had they ever had visitors. Should he call out? Theirs was the only house on the peak.

He shivered. There was something odd about the figure as it stepped through the snow. William blinked. Then he threw his hand over his mouth and let the coverlet drop to the floor. "Wha-a-t?"

It was a woman, but her arms were unnaturally long. William rubbed his eyes. Maybe she was using walking sticks? No. Her arms kinked in all directions as she used them to balance herself in the snow. William's ankles went weak.

He latched the shutter and ran to the door to be sure the bar was thrown, locking them in. He added another log to the fire. He pushed his hand through his hair. If his eyes had not tricked him, she was . . . she was like something from a bad dream. Perhaps he'd only imagined it? After all, he'd waked suddenly.

He rummaged on the worktable and found Da's small carving knife. Holding it close, he whispered to himself, *"Please, let it just be my imagination."*

There was a knock at the door.

4

chapter 2

William clutched Da's knife. They'd never worried about danger coming to them. But this—this thing he'd spied felt all wrong. It hadn't looked natural.

Thump! Thump!

Pinch mumbled in his sleep.

"Please, open the door!" said a voice. "I've journeyed a long way."

William leaned his head against the wood on his side of the door. "Who—who are you?"

"I'm a friend of your mother's, of Lirian's." The voice was pleasant.

A friend of Ma's? It would be difficult for anyone to find their home without directions from Ma or Da. Did she know where Ma was? Or, perhaps, she'd spoken with Da?

"Lirian is worried about you, William. And about your brother, Pinch. Also, I've something of hers to give you. Please let me in."

Something from Ma? This visitor *did* know where Ma was! And she knew their names. How silly he was acting. William put the knife down. He must have imagined the strange look of her. He unbarred the door. "Please, come in."

Frenzied wisps of snow whirled across the floor as she swept her gown over the threshold. She wore a gray cloak, and her hood framed a small triangle of a face. About her head tumbled pinpricks of light. She looked perfectly normal—more than normal. Certainly, she was the most beautiful person William had ever seen.

He caught his breath. "How? Who . . ." His brain was fuzzy. He was always shy around others, since he very seldom met anyone. Finally, he managed, "Good eve! I— I'm William, Heldor's son. Do you have a message from my mother?"

"Well, not exactly."

Uh-oh! Something wasn't right. She looked friendly enough, but her voice had sharpened and her eyes were cold. William moved closer to Pinch.

She smiled, and William looked up at two perfect rows of sharp little teeth. His breath rushed out. *Oh, no! Oh, no!* He'd let something dangerous into the cottage. He knew better than to open the door to a stranger,

especially when Da wasn't around. His mouth dropped open. "Wha-a-a-t—"

"Oh, quit your sniveling!" the woman snapped. "I do hate it when your sort does that."

William placed his hands on his thighs to stop his legs from shaking. He took a couple of deep breaths.

"That's better," she said. "Now raise your head and look at me. After all, I dressed for the occasion—pretty lights and all."

He raised his eyes. He could not stop staring at those teeth! "Are—are you going to eat us?"

"Am I *what*?" The stranger broke into peals of raspy laughter. Slipping off her hood, she said, "Really! How old are you?"

"Twel—twelve summers."

"Twelve summers, and you still believe in stories meant to frighten babies? Do I look like a wolf? I am *not* going to eat you."

William glanced at Pinch.

"I said, look at me!" the woman commanded. "You don't need to worry about your brother. My business is with you. Good."

She took off her gloves and slowly circled the small cottage, touching his mother's and father's things. The twinkling lights about her head moved with her. She drew a long bony finger down the blade of his father's knife.

William gulped. Who, or *what*, was she?

When she was done examining the knife, she threw back the folds of her cloak. "Now that I have your attention, let us talk. First, this is not how to welcome a guest. However, stuck in this forsaken place, it doesn't surprise me that you've not been taught any manners. You should provide a seat by the fire and something to eat."

He'd been taught manners! His hands shook as he dragged a bench closer to the hearth. Then he had to swallow a couple of times before saying, "We've—we've only got an apple, or two, left."

"Thank you," she said, sweeping her gown to one side as she sat. "Two apples, please."

William sidled around the edge of the room to pick up the apples. His stomach rumbled as he looked at them. He scuffled closer to her and held them out.

Daintily, she plucked both apples from his hands with the tips of her fingernails. "Humph! Well, I can't say I'm surprised at what lack of care you seem to have. Heldor and Lirian have not only neglected to teach you any manners, but now they're starving you. Really! Some people should never have children."

William could feel his face getting red. How dare she talk about Da and Ma like that! He clenched his hands.

She bit into one of the apples. "Pah!" She spit the bite into the fire and threw both apples into the ashes. "Nasty-tasting things! Not fresh at all."

William lurched toward the fire—maybe he could rescue the apples. She put a foot out and tripped him. He sprawled at her feet.

"There. That's better. That's where you should be when addressing the great witch of the fae folk. La Grande Morga, at your service. You may call me Morga."

He scooted around, sat up and put a hand to his head. "Witch? Fae folk?"

"Yesssss." She leaned over him, and William could smell the stink of sulfur, like rotten eggs. The lights that floated about her head began to hiss.

He squinted. The flashing lights came from flying yellow worms! And each had a tiny mouth full of teeth that snapped as the worms tumbled about her dark hair.

All of William's joints went watery. "What—what are those?"

"Do you like them? They're my pets. Grimwyrms."

William kicked out and slid backward until he was against Pinch's cot. Grimwyrms were the nightmare stuff of old tales. They weren't real. They couldn't be real!

"Don't worry, if you do exactly as I ask, they'll not harm you," Morga said. "Now, the reason I'm here is that your father was doing a small favor for me. Only"—she stopped to pull something out of a pocket—"he's met with a little accident." She held up a tuft of red hair with a yellow ribbon around it.

"That's Ma's hair. Da always carries it!" William started to thrust his hand out but quickly withdrew it.

"I told you I had a little something to give you." She dropped the lock of hair and pulled out a handkerchief to wipe her hands upon.

William jerked forward and snatched it up, clutching it to his chest. "Why—why do you have it?"

"Well, I hate to be the bearer of bad news, but it seems Heldor fell from Cliven Rock. The village folk found him at the base of the cliff and buried him in the old burial ground. I would have come sooner to tell you, but it did take a while to find this place. It is rather out of the way—"

"Agggh . . ." William pitched forward. "N-n-n-no! No! No!"

Pinch yawned and sat up in bed. "William?"

"Well, the little one is just in time for the news." Morga smiled.

"No!" William pointed a shaky finger at her. "G-g-g-go! Go away!"

"What is it?" Pinch rubbed his eyes.

William leapt from the floor and pulled his brother to his chest. "I don't believe you!"

Pinch began to cry. He pushed against William. "Let me see!"

Morga rose. "I cannot abide the sound of human blubbering. And I can see you're in no state to listen to

reason, so I'll take my leave. However, it is import.
that someone honor your father's pact and perform .
few simple tasks. So we'll meet again, when you're a little calmer. I can see myself to the door." She put on her
gloves and slowly stretched each arm out, longer and
longer.

"Who's here?" asked Pinch.

William clapped his hands firmly over Pinch's eyes.
At the door she turned and flicked a small black tongue
across her sharp teeth. "Soon," she said, and stepped
into the swirling dark.

chapter 3

The day dawned cold but calm.

William beckoned for Pinch and they made their way to the old sledge by the shed. Da had taken the good one to bring back supplies, but this one was smaller and easier to handle.

"William, the goats aren't here to pull us," Pinch said.

"I know." The goats were wintering in the lower pastures. Still, William tucked Pinch beneath hides and coverlets they'd dragged out from their beds. "I'm strong. I can pull when we can't slide." He handed his brother a metal lantern filled with embers. "Don't drop that."

"Are we going because of the bad lady in my dream?" Pinch asked.

"Dreams can't hurt you," William said, glad that Pinch had believed him when he'd said that last night had simply been a bad dream. "We're going because we're out of food. And we need to find Da. One of his friends in the village will know where he is."

William had already tucked his mother's lock of hair and his father's knife into his coat. He turned to take a last look at his home.

There was sooty writing on the outside of their door. How had he missed that just moments ago?

Pinch looked past William. "What's that?"

William sounded out the words silently. *Whiter than snow is love's light atremble. Thirteen for Morga—scooped in a thimble.* Instantly, his stomach felt queasy. *Thirteen for Morga.* Thirteen what? And did she know they were leaving?

William yanked the sledge rope.

"Wait!" Pinch called. "What's it say?"

"Nothing."

"Does, too," Pinch grumbled. "It's writing."

"It's just some sort of riddle, I guess. Or—"

"I like riddles!"

"It's not that kind of riddle. It's more of a . . ." William couldn't find the right word. Finally, he said, "It's a sort of task, I think."

"A task? Did Da write it?"

"No." William felt his heart sinking. Not Da. It was that witch. "We have to go." He pulled the sledge onto the trail.

"But who wrote it?" Pinch shouted.

"I don't know!"

Pinch stuck his thumb in his mouth.

William had no idea who this Morga was, or what Da might have been doing for her, but he did not want to be here if she showed up again. And he didn't believe Da was dead. Witches lied.

Whenever they came to an open space, William stood on the runners and they swooshed downward. But the mountain above the tree line was covered with loose shale, so it was difficult to use the sledge for sliding. For great stretches of the way, William had to pull and push it. And many times, Pinch got off and helped. It was taking longer than William expected. By midday they'd only gotten as far as the path that led off to Cliven Rock.

Cliven Rock was a boulder that teetered on the edge of a steep cliff. It was a favorite place where they sometimes went for a picnic. There they could look out upon the whole world spread before them. William had always loved the place. But now? He couldn't help picturing Da lying broken, far below. He was tempted to have a look at the ledge; maybe there would be some sign that might tell him the truth.

No. It was too dangerous in winter, especially with Pinch. And he was sure the witch had lied.

William wrapped the sledge rope tighter around his hand. He could not keep himself from glancing back. Was Morga watching them flee? Would she try to stop them? And why had she left that message on the door?

"We have to get farther down where it's warmer before we stop," he told his brother.

The wind was blowing into their faces. The gray sky revealed only a smudge where they supposed the sun to be. They struggled onward, into a world muffled by snow-fog.

Soon William spied huddled white shapes from which tips of branches poked out. A few steps later, the wind seemed to be slackening. "We're coming to the forest," he told Pinch. Finally, he could make out the gray skeletons of snow-shrouded trees.

He was strong from all the work he did, helping Da. But still, he rocked unsteadily as he painfully loosened both of his ice-encrusted hands from the rope. Catching his breath, he said, "Now that we're below the tree line, we'll stop for the night and make a fire."

Pinch squinted at the trees. "Where are we going to sleep?"

"Don't you remember what Da said to do if we ever got caught out in a snowstorm?"

Pinch started to shake his head but stopped. "He said to be a bear!"

"That's right. Tonight we'll be bears."

chapter 4

William pointed to a cluster of fir trees.
Their dense branches hung almost to the ground, except
at the rear, where they swept upward, over the face of an
embankment. He brushed aside a branch, and the musty
odor of fir needles rose. "Under there. It'll be dry."

Soon they'd kindled a small crackling fire.

"Here," William said. From the sledge he'd pulled out
a wooden bowl with two soft apples. "Um . . . these accidentally dropped in the ashes. We can still eat them."

"I'm tired of apples," Pinch complained. "Apples and
turnips. Turnips and apples."

"Well, tonight it's *just* apples. And you can have both
of them. We'll have good food when we get into the village. We just have to get to the river and follow it down
through the pastures."

While Pinch ate, William studied the ridge of snow that curved from the ledge behind them. "We need to dig a cave."

"A snow cave?" Pinch asked.

"That's right. We'll be warm, just like bears. And I'll tell you a story before we sleep."

William retrieved the spade he'd strapped to the sledge. "I'll dig. You gather some fir branches for our bed."

William tunneled in through the snow ridge. It was hard work, and he thought his arms might give out. But digging kept him warm. And soon Pinch was helping by scooping out snow with their wooden bowl.

Finally, William squinted into the cave. "Big enough." They littered the floor with branches, and over those they laid their hides and coverlets. "There!" he said. "A cozy bear den. We'll plug the opening with a big snowball. It'll be nice and warm inside."

"Do bears have bad dreams?" asked Pinch.

"I'll be right next to you. There won't be any room for bad dreams."

"There won't be any room for the bad lady?"

"No."

They let the fire die down, then pushed themselves feet-first into the cave. William studied the darkness in the forest one last time before he tugged the ball of snow they'd packed toward the cave entrance. The snowball blocked most of it. They chinked the largest gaps from the inside. Then they curled close in their hides and coverlets and were warmed by each other.

Pinch began to whimper. William found the lock of Ma's hair and held it to his own cheek a moment. Then he pressed it into Pinch's hand. "Here, hold on to this."

Pinch's whimpers softened. "It's Ma's hair! Did Da leave it with you?"

"Um . . ."

Pinch did not give him time to answer. "A story. Please?"

So William began, "Once, in good King Aethelred's time—"

"Apple-Red," said Pinch. "His name was *King Apple-Red!*"

"Sorry! I forgot."

William began again, "Once, in good King Apple-Red's time, there were three—no, *two*—bears in a cozy cave. The older bear was strong and could pull a sledge . . ."

"And he was brave!" shouted Pinch.

William smiled. "He was brave, too. And the little round-bellied bear—he was *very* special."

Pinch giggled.

chapter 5

William dreamed of being chased. In the morning, he scooted out of the cave and looked for any signs of Morga. "I don't see anyone else's footprints."

"Who else would be here?" Pinch asked.

"Ah—no one," William answered, realizing his mistake. "Help me repack."

Soon William gripped the sledge's rope and led them back over snowy hummocks until they were on the path again. There he stopped to cock an ear and sniff the air.

"What are you doing?" asked Pinch.

"Just listening and smelling. It's important to do that when you're out on your own."

Pinch sniffed and listened, too. He said, "I hear the wind, and leaves blowing."

William glanced up at the still tops of the trees. Other than the firs, the trees were bare. There were no leaves to rustle. He looked again at the evergreens. They were not swaying in the wind. Yet Pinch was right. There was a sweeping sound all around them.

William turned in circles, searching. Up the path he spied a pale yellow glow. It was not sunlight. And then he caught a whiff—sulfur. The same smell as Morga's grimwyrms.

"We have to run!" He gripped Pinch's shoulders. "Listen to me. Go as swiftly as you can. Whatever happens, don't stop. Don't wait for me if I fall down. Do you understand?"

Pinch nodded. His eyes were wide. "Wh-why?"

"Just stay on the path and run as fast as you can. Go to the very first cottage you come to and pound on the door. Leave everything." William grabbed Pinch's hand. "We can get the sledge later."

William went as quickly as he could. But he was going too fast for Pinch's short legs and had to stop often to yank his brother up by his arm. Behind them, a thick yellow fog wormed its way around the tree trunks. "We have to go faster."

He gulped; the smell was stronger. Grimwyrms, for certain! What to do . . . ? Had he brought the witch's anger down upon them by leaving? He hauled Pinch to his feet again.

"Something stinks," Pinch said.

"I know. Can't you go any faster?"

"My feet hurt."

"I'll carry you piggyback. Over there. Quick!" William pointed to a boulder, and Pinch climbed up onto it and from there onto William's back.

Pinch was heavy. Fortunately, the snow wasn't deep through the dense forest. William looked back. The yellow fog was surging closer.

"What is it?" asked Pinch.

William did not answer. He concentrated on the path ahead, trying not to trip as he huffed along. They were still not going fast enough; he'd never be able to carry Pinch very far. Should they stop and hide? He adjusted his grip on his brother as his eyes swept the nearby forest for a hiding spot.

Pinch cried out, "I'm scared. It burns!"

"I know, I know," William said. The yellow swarm carried a burning vapor with it. His throat was raw, and each breath seared him. He tried not to think about the tiny teeth he'd seen on the flying worms. William hunched forward. He staggered but kept on. Then he slammed against a sapling as they came out of the forest and into a clearing alongside the River Dightby. He reeled about.

"Ouch!" yelled Pinch. "Put me down. I can run. I promise!"

Pinch slipped from William's back, and William collapsed onto one knee, gasping to catch a clean breath. He bent forward and shook his head.

Pinch tugged on William's arm. "Get up! I can't breathe."

William raised his eyes as the grimwyrms flowed into

the clearing. The skin on his face prickled with sticki-ness. He tried to wipe it off. Then he pulled his woolen scarf up over his mouth and nose.

Pinch was clawing at his throat and trying to push his chin down into his clothes. He began to burrow beneath William.

William flailed his arms about, swatting at the first of the worms to land on them. Their stink made him want to vomit. And then he heard Pinch.

"Ow! Ow! They're biting me! Ow!"

"Pinch!" William slapped at the grimwyrms as they tore at his brother. They seemed to be spending all their rage on Pinch; although William's head and shoulders were weighted down with the creatures, they were not biting him.

William hunched over his brother, folding him up under his coat. Scooting along on his hands and knees, he crawled with Pinch to the riverbank. With one great shove, he pushed his brother into the River Dightby. Then William collapsed on the bank, rolled and fell into the icy water himself.

chapter 6

The water was milky blue with snow-melt and rock flour—and startlingly cold. "Aiii!" William was shocked back into his senses.

Pinch kicked and waved his arms. "William!"

William grabbed Pinch by the coat and tried to keep their heads above the churning water as it pitched them past logs and ice-cloaked boulders. The freezing water had cut off any thought of the grimwyrms. All William could think of was surviving the river ride and getting out. The cold Dightby could kill them just as surely as grimwyrms.

He fought to cling to his brother. Wrapping his arms around Pinch, he leaned back to keep them moving feet-first into the current. "Watch out!" William yanked up

on Pinch. They'd barely missed an underwater boulder. His brother was going limp, and their heavy clothes were dragging them down.

"C-c-c-old," Pinch whimpered.

William surveyed the banks. He knew that along the river there were plunging rapids that shot the Dightby's waters over a final high drop, Guardian's Gate, before the river calmly meandered across the valley far below.

They would die going over the falls, if the icy water didn't kill them first.

William, too, was losing strength.

He touched his toes on the rocky bottom. If he could just push them slantwise to the current . . . He flexed his knees as they floated across another boulder and then straightened his legs and pushed. They plunged backward, a little out of the main force of the river.

He sought again for some sort of grip beneath the water. The Dightby was not deep, but it was swift. And that made for missed opportunities. Yet William kept on, shoving against boulders or the rocky bottom and bouncing off to angle a little closer toward shore.

Pinch was silent. And William could barely feel his own legs, or arms.

They were approaching several blocky overhangs that signaled the upcoming rapids. William overlapped his arms, grabbing and holding fast to each elbow as he cinched his brother closer. If they went over the falls, they'd go together.

It was at that moment that his feet hit a sandbar. It rose into stiller shallows. Tugging backward, William pulled Pinch out of the main current and up onto his own chest. He lay in the calmer water, catching his breath. After a few moments, he staggered to his knees and dragged his brother to the pebble-strewn shore. There William fell.

They were free of the grimwyrms and out of the river.

But what was near the rapids? His thoughts were all muddled when he needed them to be clear. There was something he had to do. Pinch. That was it. He rolled his brother faceup. "Pinch?" He slapped Pinch's cheeks. "Pinch!"

Pinch's mouth was blue. His skin was bright red, with large purple bites from the grimwyrms. Was he breathing?

Pinch's eyelids fluttered. He *was* alive. But for how long? They would have to get somewhere warm and out of their wet clothes—or it wouldn't matter where they'd landed. Falling into the Dightby any time of year could kill a person, since its waters came from the year-round ice on Crag Angorm.

William struggled to his knees. He crawled to the gouged-out bank of the riverbed and cupped his hands. "Help! Help!" He dug into the dirt to climb up to the rim but only succeeded in sliding back down, coughing and weak.

He rolled over and stared at the opposite bank. The grasses on the far shore were frost-tipped, and they glittered like jewels in the sun. He smiled, thinking it might be a nice day.

Soon the fuzziness in his brain reminded him that there was something he needed to do. Something about Pinch. What was it? He couldn't quite . . . Where *was* Pinch, anyway? He ran his hands over his chest. Why were his clothes wet?

He was all mixed up. He yawned. Then he had an idea. Maybe he'd close his eyes—just for a little. He'd rest. Then he'd be able to think. Just . . . just for a moment . . . he'd close . . . his eyes.

William opened his eyes. *Pinch?* He clutched at his side and strained to sit up. He failed. Every muscle in his body ached. He lay still a moment, gulping in warm air. He was in a room with a thatched ceiling. The rafters above were hung with herbs, and all around were shelves overflowing with vials, boxes and bundles.

Where was Pinch? He took another breath and pushed himself onto one hip. His knees knocked against each other. Not from cold. He shook from weakness and . . . something else. What if Pinch wasn't here?

He remembered looking at the sunlight by the river. He remembered closing his eyes. He remembered thinking it was too beautiful a day to die. Had he let his brother die?

chapter 7

William forced his eyes to focus. "Ah . . . Pinch." Pinch was in the room. William squeezed his eyes closed and reopened them—just to make sure. Yes! His brother was sleeping on the floor. William gave in to a coughing fit.

The next time William woke, he could smell honey. And there was a warmth here that was so familiar, so comfortable. "Ma!" he murmured, and happiness sprang up in his chest.

He opened his eyes and tried to throw off the heavy coverlets. He couldn't; for some reason, he was weak. He didn't understand. He wanted to run to his mother, but when he moved he ended up shaking and coughing. Blearily, it came to him that this wasn't home. Yet there was something vaguely familiar . . . He glanced at the jumbled shelves. Where was he? How did he get here?

There was something about being chased and a river . . . and Pinch! Pinch had been attacked by flying worms.

"Pinch! P—" William's voice cracked. The room went spinning downward. He caught himself and leaned over just as he vomited onto the floor.

Taking long slow breaths, he pushed back the blankets. He *had* to get up. Had his brother died in the river? No. No, he didn't think so. He remembered seeing Pinch before he'd drifted off to sleep. But where was he now? The pallet on the floor was empty. Had he died during the night? *"Pinch!"* William yelled.

"Such clatter-wailing! I swear," mumbled a large gray-haired woman as she pushed aside the curtain that served as one wall of the room. She wiped her hands on a rag. "It's enough to roust the haunts out of the burying ground."

"Burying ground? Is Pinch dead?"

"Coo and stumpifications!" complained the woman. "That's not what—"

But that was as far as she got before a lumpy head appeared at her side. Pushing past her skirts, Pinch cried, "William, you should see what Moggety's got. Look!" His brother dumped two kittens, an orange and a gray tabby, onto the bed.

"Pinch." William swallowed hard, his whole body collapsing with relief. "Look—look at you! Your head is swollen, and you've got bites all over you."

"It doesn't hurt a lot." Pinch touched his face. "Moggety put salve on me."

"It's frightful looking, but he'll heal," the woman said. "And thanks be, he didn't get any worse than that. My medicine will bring the swelling down. But it can't take out all the poisons those beasties have in their mouths. It may still bother him for a tad."

"I was afraid . . . Ouch!" William yelped as one of the kittens leapt from his leg onto the floor. It landed in the watery puddle he had vomited.

"Now, look at that. Both of you will need a bathing-up, I reckon," said the woman.

"I'm—I'm sorry, Mistress—" William rallied his strength to get control of the remaining kitten and tried to remember whether she'd told him who she was. He began to stutter, "I—I—I'm Will—"

"I'm Moggety," she cut in. "And you . . . you're in a sorry state!"

"I—" William started to say something else but couldn't remember what it was. His head felt woozy. And somehow, he had hold of an orange bundle of energy that he had no idea what to do with.

"I can take her." Pinch gathered up the orange kitten while Moggety rescued the gray one.

"You rest a wee bit longer, and I'll brew some tea to settle that stomach soon as I take care of this bit o' bother."

William wasn't sure if the *bit o' bother* was the mess he'd made on the floor or the ooze-soaked gray kitten. He didn't have time to think about it, because Pinch crawled onto the bed with the remaining cat.

"Are you sure you're all right?" William lightly touched his brother's cheek.

"I didn't like those bitey bugs. And they stunk!

Moggety said it was a good thing you pushed me in the river, or they might have chewed me right up!" Pinch shivered. Then he held up the orange kitten. "Guess what I call her? Lirian! And the gray one is Heldor."

William frowned. "You can't call them by Ma and Da's names."

"Can, too! Moggety said I could name them whatever I wanted. And this one is almost the color of Mama's hair. They're Lirian and Heldor. So there," Pinch said, just as Lirian stretched out a paw and swatted William on the chin.

Then Pinch turned his back so he had the kitten all to himself. "Besides, those're only their baby names. They have to grow into their real names yet, just like me."

William started to tell his brother that pets didn't get two names the way people did, but he was too tired to protest. He yawned. There was still something bothering him.

There'd been a misshapen witch, Morga. She'd come to the peak with her grimwyrms. She'd started all this. And now? Now that Pinch was safe, he needed to find Da.

Da . . . William shoved his fist into his mouth. He wanted his father. The witch had said Da was dead—that he'd fallen from Cliven Rock. But that couldn't be. Da would never go there in the winter. William didn't believe it. Still, he pulled the covers over his head.

"William? William?" Pinch put a chubby arm around him and held on.

chapter 8

Moggety returned with a freshly wiped-down kitten.

William untangled Pinch from around his neck and tried to rise from the bed. "Do you know our da?" he asked. "Heldor, from up on the peak."

"Crumpelstilts!" said Moggety. "You're not fit to be moving about. Keep your head down." She handed the gray kitten to Pinch. Then she proceeded to clean the floor. All William could see was her huge square backside rearing up as she knelt.

"But what about our father? We're looking for him," William said.

Pinch added, "He didn't come home."

"Aye! I know him," Moggety said, harrumphing as she got to her feet. "But you need to rest now. We'll chat soon." Moggety nodded toward Pinch, who'd put his thumb in his mouth. "Just you and me, Master William."

William looked at his brother's big eyes. If she didn't want to talk in front of Pinch, perhaps the witch *had* told the truth. "Take your thumb out of your mouth," he snapped.

Pinch did, and stuck his tongue out at William.

Moggety said, "I've all your clothes washed out and dried. And there's some special whatnots of yours in yon box."

Ma's lock of hair and Da's knife were safe! William turned to study his brother. "Your face is swollen, but why aren't you as beat up from the river as I am?"

"Oh," cut in Moggety, putting her hands on her hips. "The wee ones are more bendable-like. The Dightby is not so hard on them as on older folk. But you've not gotten the full force of the river, either. I've rescued others that have fared worse."

Moggety pushed back the curtain to reveal the other half of her home. On the hearth was a pot. She stooped to stir something that smelled like vegetables and sweet herbs. "That's one of my jobs," she said. "And I've not missed a body that should be plucked out."

William was surprised someone actually had such a job. And were there some folks who *shouldn't* be rescued? He wanted to ask.

But just then Pinch piped up, "Moggety's the guardian."

"What?"

"You know," Pinch said. "Moggety's the guardian at the falls."

"I thought Guardian's Gate was just the name of the falls. I didn't know there was an actual . . ." William's voice trailed off.

"I'm a simple herb-wife," Moggety said. "But aye! I do guard the Dightby and other things. Just in case." She winked.

"Thank you for rescuing us." William yawned. "I think I'd better rest some more," he added. "I—I feel weak."

"Do that," Moggety said, "and we'll have us a nice supper later."

That evening, she ladled chunky soup into small-bowled piggins and handed them around. William didn't touch his right away. He asked, "What if people fall in close to the falls?"

Moggety nodded toward the door. Then she opened it as William sat his piggin down and rose to step slowly over the rush-strewn floor. "See yon space where the rock on both sides narrow down to a wee arm's width?"

William had to look up to see the top of the huge chunk of stone that overhung the River Dightby's sudden descent into the falls. He could just make out a small gap. "Yes."

"They call that Mog's Skinny. If I miss someone upriver, then I get a long-crooked pole down at that point. Nary a miss yet!"

"How do you know when someone's coming down the river?"

"I've got my ways."

"How did you get to be the guardian?"

"Ach! Well, that's a longish tale and your soup's waiting. Let's just say that there be some as care about the world we can see and feel all about us, and some as care about the unseen world. And I'm one of the caretakers of the seen world. Now, let's get some food into you, shall we?"

William didn't quite understand what she'd just said, but he studied her a moment. Her curly gray hair was stuffed up under a gathered cap. The sleeves of her woven overblouse were rolled above her elbows, revealing strong freckled arms. And there was something familiar about her.

He was just going to ask if they'd met before when she said, "You'd best finish your supper while it's hot."

After they had eaten, Pinch laid his cheek alongside William's arm. "What were those things that bit me?" he asked. "How come you didn't get bit?"

William shuddered. "I don't know why I didn't get bit. But those things might be"—his voice dropped—"grimwyrms."

Pinch's face fell. "Were not! There's no such thing." He punched William in the side.

"Oooo! Not a pretty subject for the likes of such a glorious evening," interrupted Moggety.

William pushed Pinch's small fist away and put his arm around his brother. He said to Moggety, "I thought . . . well, I always thought they weren't *really* real. I thought grimwyrms were just imaginings. You know, from bad dreams or old stories."

"They're as much gristle and bone as you," she said. "Ofttimes, things that have a claw-hold in our dreams have another in the real world. And don't be so quick to dismiss the old tales. They're full of wonders it just takes a special way of looking at to understand. Now, those things . . . ach! Those grimwyrms have daggerous teeth. If they were sent after you, it was a powerful sending."

Pinch tried to crawl into his brother's lap, but his hands were over his ears.

William helped him up and glanced toward the door. He wanted to run and slide the bar across. He tightened his arm around Pinch. "A sending? What's that? And why would those things be after us?"

chapter 9

"**H**o!" Moggety yelped. "For certain, there's no mystery about that last question. They were hankering to feast on you. And a sending is . . . well, that's a bit harder to explain." She drummed her fingers on the tabletop. "Did you ever, when you were completely by yourself, somehow feel that you *weren't* by yourself?"

"I'm not sure," William said. Then he remembered waking and feeling as if his mother was there. "I guess so. Sometimes."

"Well, that's a kind of sending," Moggety said. "When there's a strong feeling between folks, good or bad, that"—she fumbled for a word—"that *pull* can be tied to something evil, or something good. If the person doing the sending is good, it's a good sending that finds you. If the body doing the sending is evil, and that person is powerful, then bad things can come."

Moggety propped an elbow on the table. "Hmm . . . I can only think of one person strong enough to send down a whole horde of those nasties. And I'd wager it was her doing. Hah! That is, if I was a wagering woman." She slapped the tabletop and laughed.

William couldn't understand why Moggety seemed to be in a happy mood. Getting visited by Morga and attacked by grimwyrms was nothing he'd laugh about. He was about to tell her so when Pinch took his hands off his ears and piped up.

"I saw a bad lady once! At our house. But she was sent in a dream."

Moggety's eyes widened. She glanced at William with what seemed like a question in them.

Behind Pinch, William nodded.

"I see . . . ," she said.

William tried to change the subject. "Do you know what's happened to our—"

Moggety raised a hand and stopped him. "Enough of this. Sure we're in need of more pleasant tales, especially for the young one, seeing as how the sun is slipping away."

"Yes, a story!" said Pinch, wiggling around in William's lap.

Despite the heat from the fire, William shivered. All

this talk of bad sendings was making him uneasy. "Yes!" he agreed.

Moggety clapped her hands. "Good! It's been an owl's age since I've had any young ones to entertain. Let's see . . . shall it be the tale of brave King Aethelred and the Ooliphant Beast, or Princess Bree and the Haeftling Dragon?"

"Princess Bree!" shouted Pinch. "William already told me a story about King Apple-Red, when we slept in a bear cave."

Moggety burst out laughing. "Apple-Red! That's a right name for him. I've heard tell that Aethelred was a very round man, and his cheeks were as red as apples. But King Ael . . . er, *Apple-Red* can wait for another night. Now," she continued, "make yourselves comfortable."

"Wait." Pinch slipped from William's lap and picked up the two kittens. "Lirian and Heldor want to hear, too."

Moggety laughed again and got up to poke at the fire. She stirred until a tiny tongue of flame battled back the darkness. It made for a snug arena in which to hear the adventures of Princess Bree.

In a short while Pinch's eyelids began to droop, and he slumped against his brother—having long ago surrendered the kittens to their evening explorations. Moggety raised a finger. "Shh . . . let's tuck the wee one in proper-like, and then we must talk, Master William.

About Morga. You've met her, I fear." For a moment, she looked as if she wanted to spit angrily.

"Yes. She came to the cottage. That was one of the reasons we left. And she wrote a message on our door, but I don't know what it means."

Moggety grimaced at that. Then she lifted the sleeping Pinch into her arms and carried him beyond the curtain wall. William heard her tucking his brother in for the night.

When she returned, she stood by William and laid her hand lightly upon his shoulder. "First, the important thing. I heard about your father. I'm so sorry. Heldor was a good man, and a friend."

William began to shake. "Then . . ." He gulped. "Then it's true? He's . . . he's dead?"

"Yes." She leaned down to wrap her arms around his shoulders. "It's true."

William gave in and cried for a long time.

Later, he was left to his thoughts while Moggety tidied up for the night. He huddled by the fire, hugging his knees. *Da is dead.* But it didn't make any sense. Da wouldn't have gone up to Cliven Rock when the ledge was snow-covered and slippery.

William tugged a strand of his hair and began to twist it. That was when he saw Moggety by the fire. Somehow, she'd walked past him without his noticing.

"You wanted to talk about Morga?" he said. "She came in the middle of the night to our cottage."

He tried to clear his thoughts. "It wasn't just a bad dream Pinch had. I made that up. She was really there, and she told me Da died. Who, or what, is she?"

The woman did not answer; she sat with her back to him. Using a poker, she stirred the ashes of the dying fire and muttered to herself.

William's throat tightened whenever a reflection from the fire winked against a glass vial on a shelf. The flickering seemed like eyes blinking: open . . . shut. He yawned. Then he pursed his lips and shook himself.

"Moggety?" he asked. "Morga said Da had been helping her. And there was writing on our door. Do you know what it means?"

There was no answer. "Moggety?" he said, more loudly. "What about the witch?"

Without turning from the fire, the woman chanted. Her voice was hypnotizing as it lulled in the plump music of an older language. He closed his eyes . . . and he understood.

> *Whiter than snow.*
> *Redder than blood.*
> *Blacker than night.*
>
> *A thimble of love.*
> *A handful of flame.*
> *A spindle of death.*
> *And I'll go whence I came.*

He opened his eyes. The woman was gone. But little tongues from the burning coals beckoned. He crawled toward the fire and stretched out a hand. *A handful of flame . . .*

"Here!" Moggety grabbed William around the middle and yanked him backward. "Great jack-n-abouts! What are you up to?"

"I—" William stared at his hand. "What?"

"I asked, what were you doing? You almost crawled into the hot coals. It's a good thing I was gone but a twinkling." Moggety felt his forehead. "Why, you're as damp as the Dightby River!" She got him to his feet. "To bed with you. What I have to say can wait."

"But you *were* talking. By the fire, in a strange language. And I understood! There's—there's something I must do. Only . . ." He tried to twist around and look at her face, but a wave of dizziness swept over him. "Only, I can't remember what it is."

"Was I?" Moggety asked. "There by the fire this whole time? Humph! And how do you reckon the last wood for the night got fetched? I've been out and about. It's to bed with you, or you'll catch your death."

"You *were* there," he said as Moggety helped him into bed. "I thought—" He yawned. "I thought you were saying something about the fire. I was supposed to catch it in my hand. Maybe it was a dream." He threw his arm up over his forehead. "Maybe it was one of those . . . a . . . a sending?" he mumbled.

"Shh . . ." She hushed him. And for a long time she stroked his hot cheek.

chapter 10

*T*hump! "Stumpifications!" The uproar beyond the curtain startled William. Groggily, he lifted his head. Already day was sliding into dusk.

Something coppery flashed across the floor. Then Pinch threw back the curtain. "There you are!" Pinch said, grabbing Lirian. "She knocked over one of Moggety's bottles. And Heldor's hiding."

William rubbed his eyes. "He'll come out when it's calmer." He pushed himself up. "Your head is not so swollen, and the bite marks have scabbed over."

"Moggety bathed my head in salve again. It smells like honey. But sometimes I get dizzy."

"You'll feel better soon." William's mind had cleared, but he felt shaky. "Can you help me?"

Pinch helped his brother get dressed. "I think Lirian

knocked Moggety's bottle over on purpose." He lowered his voice. "It stinks."

William raised an eyebrow. "There *is* something that doesn't smell good." He ducked past the curtain wall.

Moggety was busy at a shelf by the casement that opened out onto the front garden. Despite the crisp weather, she had the shutter open. Whatever she was trying to clear away stank like rotten potatoes.

Moggety turned from her work. "And a glorious good eve to you!" she said. "I see you are upright, with a fine color to your cheeks."

"I feel better. Just wobbly. About last night, you were telling me there was something I had to do. Something about fire. I can't remember it all."

Moggety's smile became a hard line. "Later." Then, smiling again, she said, "Can one of you keep those fire-breathing botherations out from under my feet?"

"Fire-breathing?" Pinch said.

William looked from Moggety to Lirian, who was sitting just outside the open door in the flickering gold of twilight. The cat was bathing a hind leg that was daintily lifted over her head.

"One never knows what might be a haeftling dragon," Moggety said with a wink.

That night, Moggety told the boys the tale of how brave King Aethelred rode an ooliphant beast out of the

Southlands. When she'd finished, Pinch said, "I wish I had an ooliphant."

William nudged him with his shoulder. "What would you do with one?"

"I'd ride him all the way to Da. And he'd help us find Mama." Pinch swiped at his nose.

William scowled. He hadn't, yet, told Pinch about their father. "I've been thinking about that. I'm feeling better. We need to—*I*," he corrected himself, "need to see if I can find Ma."

"And Da, too!" Pinch added.

William squeezed his lips together.

Moggety said, "I've a thought, or two, about your mother—"

"You do?" William interrupted. "Do you know—"

"In the morn." Moggety raised a hand. "I need to get my thoughts all sorted out. Right now, I've an inkling that there is something the wee one should know. And I'm thinking that while we're all snug-like, now might be a good time." With that, Moggety swept Pinch onto her lap and ran a hand lightly over his head, ruffling his hair.

"What?" asked Pinch. He looked at both of them a moment, then slipped his thumb into his mouth.

William didn't bother to tell him to take it out. He gripped the edge of the bench. Moggety was right; he had to tell Pinch. But to say the words! It felt like drowning. He tried to push down the panic flooding up from his heart. He leaned forward. "Pinch . . . Da is dead."

chapter 11

"**H**e is not! You lie!" Da wasn't dead, Pinch insisted. Then he collapsed against William, his wails filling the little house. Later, Pinch fell into a sweaty sleep, sucking his thumb.

William tossed and turned all night. The next morning, he was up early—before Pinch. He and Moggety sat at the table.

"William, there was evil here the other eve." Moggety kept her voice low. "It was not me, speaking to you."

William leaned in. "It wasn't? Then who?"

Moggety shook her head. "It was a sending of Morga's. You said the witch came to your cottage?"

"Yes! And I . . ." William rubbed the back of his neck. "I let her in! She said she was a friend of Ma's and had something for us. I thought she might know where Ma was. But I know better than to open a door to a stranger." He gulped. "I opened the door. It was . . . so, so stupid of me. I—"

"Shh," Moggety said. "Don't go beating yourself about it. She's a tricky one, and she'd have gotten in some way. No one invited her in, this time. Yet she got in here, in my own place, with a sending. Now, what did she say while she was up at your cottage?"

"She said Da . . . Da had died. But I didn't believe her." William's voice caught in his throat. "She said he was doing a favor for her when he fell. And Da had entered into a pact with her that someone had to honor. But I don't know what she was talking about."

Moggety rubbed at her elbows. "I don't know the whole story of that hag. But I do know that any daughter of the fairy lands will not give up till she gets what she wants—especially a thirteenth daughter of a thirteenth daughter, as she is.

"I did warn Heldor about that when he came to me for help in trying to untangle some foolish riddle she'd told him. Oh, the fae folk and their riddles!" Moggety shook her head. "One would think they'd be plainspoken, if it be about something they want. Let's see . . ." She tapped the tabletop. "There was a bit about *whiter than snow*. I remember that, but—"

"That's what was written on the door!" William closed his eyes and recited, *"Whiter than snow is love's light atremble. Thirteen for Morga—scooped in a thimble."*

"Aye, that sounds like it. Well, 'tis certain she wants

something of you, as she did of Heldor. But know this, the only way he'd do anything for that fae witch would be if she threatened the two of you, or your mother."

"Ma!" William leaned closer. "You said you might have an idea about where she is."

"I've fears she might be in the Old Forest. The Dightby flows along its southern border, and I've felt something odd from the river for the last year or so. Something's not right. I've not seen anything with my own eyes, mind you. But Heldor went that way more than once. That I know."

William jumped up. "Then I have to go, too! If she's there, I'll find her."

"Hush now, don't go waking the little one. The Old Forest is a goodly distance. You'll need things. And how're you going to get there? It's a long walk on two feet."

"You said Da went there. And he was never gone for too many days in a row. I can go—"

"Go where?" Pinch asked sleepily as he pushed past the curtain wall.

"Nowhere," said William.

Pinch screwed his face up in disbelief. "Is *too* somewhere. I know it. If you're going somewhere, I'm going, too." Pinch's voice was rising.

"Shh! I need to find Ma. You can't come. You'd slow me down."

"Would not! I'm fast. Watch!" Pinch ran in circles. He almost knocked over the bench, and the kittens scrambled up onto shelves, their fur standing on end.

"No!" William said.

Pinch's lip jutted out. He flung himself on the floor. "Don't go! What if . . . what if you don't come back?"

William knelt down. He could feel Pinch's fear as his brother wrapped his arms about his neck and sobbed. After a while, he said, "You want me to find Ma, don't you?"

"Yes." Pinch nodded, wiping at his nose. "But I could help. I'm good at finding. I always find the kittens."

"I'll have to travel a long way. I can't take the sledge; we left it in the forest. Besides, there's no snow in the valley. You can stay here with Moggety. The kittens need you to care for them."

"I could carry them," Pinch pleaded.

William shook his head. "No. It may be too dangerous for little kittens. And your face and head are not healed yet. You need to keep salve on those bites."

Pinch crossed his arms. "Then I'm going to stay *right here* in the middle of the floor until you get back. I'm not moving! I'm not even going to move a single toe!"

William rolled his eyes.

chapter 12

William tucked his father's knife and
the lock of his mother's hair into a pocket. Moggety had
already packed some food, a goatskin of cider and a bedroll for him. He'd looped a piece of twine loosely about
the bedroll and used that to slip his arms through. The
pack rode securely on his back.

Moggety handed the lantern full of live coals to him.
"Stay on the towpath west of the village. The Old Forest borders the river. There are boats on the Dightby;
perhaps you can get a ride to the forest. Beyond, I do
not know."

"What if . . ." William licked his lips. "What if those—
those things are still there? Grimwyrms?"

"It's nigh impossible to keep a sending about for a
longish time. But there may be other troubles. Morga,"

Moggety said. "She believes she had some sort of pact with your father. Solemn pledges are important to the fae folk. That means she'll try to get at you again."

William's heart quickened its beat. Still, he stiffened his legs and patted her hand where it lay upon his arm. "I'll be fine. Da taught me how to take care of myself."

"Aye. But I have something as may help a wee bit." Moggety pulled up on a silver chain she wore about her neck. On the chain hung a tiny blue vial with a cork stopper. She pulled the chain over her head and held the vial a long time in her hands. At last, she said, "I've no idea if this'll help. But it's something I've carried next to my heart." Then she dropped the long chain over William's head.

He picked up the miniature vial. "What's in it?"

Moggety gave him a smile. "Something from someone who once loved me as the dearest prize of his life. Imagine that!" She chuckled as she tucked it down inside his shirt. "Keep it safe. It may help me to send you good thoughts."

"Good sendings?"

She nodded. "I'll try, but I'm a bit rusty. And do remember to bring it back."

"I will." He placed his hand over the spot where the cool glass of the tiny bottle rested against his chest. He rose and hugged Moggety. Then he ducked past the curtain to say good-bye to Pinch.

His little brother had spent the previous day refusing to move from the middle of the floor. But last night he'd allowed Moggety to tuck him into bed.

William put his hand on the small lump under the covers and found Pinch's shoulder. He squeezed it. "I have to go, Pinch. I'll find Ma and bring her home." William bit his lip. He'd only been separated from Pinch a few times. And that was only when his mother had taken Pinch on her back and hiked down to the mountain when his brother was just a baby.

"Promise me you'll behave. That you'll listen to Moggety and be good."

Pinch wiggled a little, and the gray kitten came out from under the coverlets, stretched and walked off. "I'm always good," Pinch mumbled.

"I know. It's just . . . it's just that I'm going to miss you, that's all."

Pinch threw back the covers and sat up. "Then take me with you."

"You know I can't."

"I know! I'm just a baby. I don't even have a real name yet." Pinch plopped back and yanked the coverlets up again.

Moggety came to William's side. "I'll keep an eye on the wee one. We'll tell lots of good tales while you're gone. I've got more of King Aethel . . . *Apple-Red* up my sleeve, as well as Princess Bree."

William nodded and went to the door. When he looked back, he saw Pinch peeking at him. He waved.

Pinch sat up and lifted his arms to Moggety. "I want Da!"

"Coo, lovey! A course you do," she said. Then she lifted William's little brother and held him.

William shut the door and leaned his head against the rough wood. What choice did he have but to leave Pinch? There could be dangers on the road ahead. He pushed his shoulders back and straightened his pack. It was time to go.

The path to the valley was steep. Nearby, the falls spewed water over slabs of rock in the pool at their foot. William marveled at the thunderous downpouring and was thankful that they'd gotten out before the falls.

When he came to a meadow, he stopped to rest against a red and silver lichened boulder. His breath made small clouds in the cold air. The sun was well up and throwing shadows. He searched the trail behind him for any sign of a yellow mist. Nothing. No movement . . . wait! What was that flicker?

William bent his knees and crouched on the damp ground behind the boulder. He peered around the rock. Nothing now. He swiveled back, tilted his face into the sun and chewed at his lip. If he stood up he'd be exposed. But he couldn't sit there all day, either.

He leaned around and looked again. Yes! There was a movement.

Who could be following him? Morga? What to do? Then he heard the laughter—raspy and deep—above his head!

chapter 13

William caught a whiff of sulfurous breath. He tilted his head back. The witch was leaning over the boulder. She waggled her fingers at him.

He lunged forward and pushed himself to his feet.

"Don't tell me I surprised you! Poor me. I'm always unexpected. I do remember making quite a wonderful stir, once, at a royal celebration. It was so much fun!"

The fae witch pulled her cloak tighter. William noticed that her arms were a normal length. And at first glance, she looked young and lovely.

"I did tell you we'd meet again," she added. "And it wasn't very friendly to rush off like that! Just when I thought it might be nice to have another visit up at your quaint home."

Morga lifted a hand and pointed back to the trail. "Did you know you were being followed?"

"What?" William looked from her to the shadowed path. "I thought it was you."

"Well, it's not me. But do come along; I think you'll find this interesting." She motioned with her hand. "Come," she said as he hesitated.

William followed. A short distance up the trail, she moved aside so he could see. And what he saw was— "Pinch!" His brother lay sprawled, his eyes rolled back. Nearby was a cinched pouch that wiggled and mewled.

William cradled his brother's head. "Wake up!" He shook Pinch's shoulders. He looked up at Morga. "What's wrong with him? Did you do something to him?"

"He really does not look well." Morga *tsk*ed. "Aren't you supposed to be caring for your brother?" She regarded William with a look of rebuke. "Really, I'm sure your parents would not at all approve of your sloppiness! It seems he had to stop and munch a few *very* early berries that happened to appear just as his tiny tummy was growling. Human children have no self-control."

William was shaking. It was *all* his fault. If he hadn't let Morga into their house, this wouldn't have happened. Da always said that once you opened the door to evil, there was hardly any way to sweep it out again. And that was exactly what William had done! He'd opened the door to evil, and now Pinch was paying the price for his stupidity. William swallowed dryly and asked, "Is he going to die?"

Morga lifted an eyebrow. "Who knows? His bites are healing. But there's still some poison in them. Combined with the berries . . . Well, I'd have to say the chances are not great that he'll live. Unless . . ."

"Unless?" Heat rose to William's neck and cheeks. He stood and faced her. "Unless!"

"Well, first of all, that quack Moggety can't heal him. Her potions are nothing more than *stink-swills* and a dash of misplaced hope. So . . ." The fae witch tapped a finger on her chin and continued. "Either he will die, or you will do me a favor by performing a couple of *itsy-*

bitsy tasks. Then I will make him well, and we can all live happily ever after!" She gave a little clap.

William could hear Pinch's chest rattling as it rose and fell. Pinch's eyelids flickered over the ghostly whites of his eyes. William went down on his knees again and put a hand on Pinch's cheek. Without looking up at Morga, he said, "Make him better."

"All right, I can do that. But you've only heard a bit about the favor I need; there's much more. I really do need you to pledge wholeheartedly to it, or it's just not going to turn out well."

Now William felt heat coursing through him. It filled up the places where he'd only felt a sickly weakness before. He didn't know much about other people, but he did know kindness—and meanness—when he saw it. He twisted around and glared at her. "You—you like playing with people! It's evil. But I won't let him die."

"Oh! You've got gumption! You may come in handy after all," Morga replied. Then she moved toward the pouch that lay nearby. "Something stinks," she said, and raised a foot to kick the bag.

"Stop that! Those are just kittens."

"Are you sure? They smell like some ancient dreck I can't stand."

"Yes." William picked up the pouch. It squirmed in his hands. He laid it down by Pinch's side and turned to the witch. "I know what you want."

"You do?"

"Yes. We read your message on our door. *Whiter than snow is love's light atremble. Thirteen for Morga—scooped in a thimble.* You want a thimble of—of sunlight, or—"

"Hah!" She snorted. "Don't be a fool, like your father was. Who would want a thimble of sunlight?"

William felt his face flush. He clenched his fists. "My father was *not* a fool! You killed him, didn't you?"

Morga threw her hands up in the air. "I've been on this earth for hundreds of years, and still the stupidity of humanity amazes me. Of course I didn't kill him!" She began to stride back and forth, waving her arms. "The idiot slipped and fell, trying to . . . to catch sunbeams, or something, off Cliven Rock, because that was a spot where your mother loved the light. But I ask you"—she stopped her pacing—"who in his right mind would do that? Especially in winter, when it's treacherous. Really! I thought he had more sense. Now, I don't want *you* to go to waste on a stunt like that. There aren't many left in your family. Just you and that whiny Pinch." She pointed at his brother. "And he's too young to do what needs to be done."

"Leave my brother out of your plans."

She approached him, so close he could smell the stink of her breath. "*Someone* must fulfill the promise your father made. And if you do not, one day I'll come for Pinch, and he will." She stepped back from William and sighed. "So I suppose that means I will have to heal him—in case you fail me."

She shook her head. "And really, he needs a true name. You should give him one. Your father's dead. No use waiting any longer. And your mother? Well, she's no help to anyone."

"My mother?" Without thinking, William stepped closer to her. "What . . . about . . . my . . . mother? What's happened to her? Tell me!" he shouted, surprising himself. He'd never yelled at anyone other than Pinch.

"Oh, don't worry." Morga waved him away. "She's in a safe place in the Old Forest. You can't miss her. She's protected by a magical barrier, put there by my sweet but empty-headed sisters. Pah! Idiots, all of them. Anyway, the barrier is a problem for me. And she has something of mine that I want back. She stole it."

"My mother is not a thief!" Her talk was making his head feel woozy.

"Oh, all right! Perhaps she *accidentally* took it. But the point is, I want it back."

"What—" That was all William got out before he heard Pinch groan. He knelt.

Pinch's pupils were visible in his eyes again.

"Ahh, poor Pinch," Morga said. "I can heal him, if you're willing to help me."

William whirled to face her. "What do you want?" he cried. "Just tell me what you want and be done with it!"

"I want my toy. And your mother has it."

chapter 14

A **toy? William clutched his head. He**
spluttered, "A . . . t-t-t-oy?"

"Oh, don't be like that. It's really more of an *heir-loom* than a toy. It's been in our family for generations, and *I'm* the one who lost track of it. Or had it stolen. Anyway," she rushed on, "I need your help. You see, my thirteenth daughter's thirteenth name-day celebration is coming up, and I want to give it to her as a present. So I'm willing to make a bargain. You promise to help me, and I'll help Pinch. What could be fairer than that?"

William pressed his fingers against his forehead. He heard Pinch's ragged breathing.

Morga broke into his thoughts. "Or," she said, with a tilt of her head and a fluttering of her eyelashes, "I could invite my flying friends to come and dine on Pinch again, just a little bit more. I wouldn't want to actually kill him, after all. Also, I happen to know that grimwyrms like the taste of kittens."

William rocked back on his heels. "No! Don't hurt him anymore. Y-yes. I'll help you get your toy!"

"You *solemnly* vow to help me get it?"

"Yes, I vow! Now, help Pinch."

"Good! Your oath is accepted. And about that full thimble, it's of love's light, *not* sunlight that someone loves—"

William interrupted her. "First, you promised to help Pinch!"

Morga swept haughtily around him. "Well, this won't be as much fun." She bent over his brother. And then, with a shrug, she produced a flagon from within her cloak. She dumped the contents of it over Pinch's head.

"Stop that!" William roared, and without thinking, he pushed her bare hands aside. "Aiii!" His palms burned as if they were covered with liquid fire. His eyes watered and he bit his lips as he knelt by Pinch, mopping his brother up. "What are you doing? He'll freeze."

Morga was bent in half, clutching her hands. Her face was screwed up tightly. "Don't worry," she muttered. "He'll feel better soon."

There was a strange unsettled quality to her voice, but William didn't have long to wonder about it. In this cold weather, it was important that he dry Pinch off quickly. He did notice that the cool wetness of what she'd poured over his brother seemed to soothe his own burning hands. He glanced over his shoulder. "He'd better heal," he said. "Or I won't help you find your toy."

She uncurled and shrieked at him. "You will! You've given an oath." She made a hissing noise. Then several floating yellow lights rose from the darkness of her cloak to shine about her. Grimwyrms!

William threw himself over his brother. They did not attack.

Morga laughed. "I've kept my end of the bargain. He will heal. And I've told you where to find your mother, so the two of you can be reunited. Now"—she pointed a bony finger at him—"I expect you to keep *your* promise to get my toy. If you don't, I'll come for Pinch and make sure he suffers."

William's whole body shook. What had he gotten into?

"Here's what you must do," Morga said. "*All of it,* and then I can get my heirloom. Look at me! I haven't time to waste. The writing on your door was only the first task. Listen well to all the tasks!"

William sat up and watched as she whirled, her cloak floating out. She chanted:

> *Whiter than snow is love's light atremble.*
> *Thirteen for Morga—scooped in a thimble.*

Redder than blood are flames that will brand.
Thirteen for Morga—clutched in bare hand.

Blacker than night is death's icy kindle.
Thirteen for Morga—fixed on a spindle.

A thimble of love.
A handful of flame.
A spindle of death.
And I'll go whence I came.

William pressed his hands against his chest as the words were seared onto his heart. He blinked, and she was gone.

Pinch groaned. "William?"

"Yes? Yes!" William lifted his brother's head. "Do you feel better? What can I do for you? How's your tummy?"

"I don't feel so good," Pinch mumbled. "I—I ate some berries and fell down. Then the bad woman came."

"I know. Here. Sit up. Drink some of Moggety's cider. Are you cold? Do you want my coat? Where do you hurt?"

"All over." Pinch's lip trembled. "I'm sorry. I know I was supposed to stay with Moggety. Are you mad?"

William hugged Pinch.

"Ouch!"

Gently, William placed his forehead against Pinch's. He left it there for a long moment. "No, I'm not mad. Just . . . just relieved. But"—William leaned back, lifted his brother's cap and knuckle-rubbed Pinch's head—"don't ever eat anything that's growing wild unless Moggety, or I, tell you that you can. And don't ever, *ever* disobey me again."

Pinch nodded. "I won't. And Lirian and Heldor won't, either."

"Oh! I almost forgot about them." William picked up the pouch. A furry gray leg protruded from the sack.

chapter 15

That night, Pinch was put to bed with a dose of something smelly from a brown bottle.

Moggety said, "I'm not sure what kind of berries he's eaten. But they don't seem to be twisting his innards up now. And even the bites of those nasties are starting to fade." She sat at the table. "I'm so sorry!" She stretched her hands toward William. "I don't know how the scamp got past me. One minute he was sitting by the door, and the next minute he was gone." She snapped her fingers. "Mark my words, there's more to this than a child simply wandering off. I'll sort this out when the wee one can tell me more. But you've not told me your whole tale yet."

"She had grimwyrms with her. Morga promised to make Pinch well. I thought he was going to die." William squeezed his lips shut and shivered.

"You must have promised her something in exchange. That's the only way that creature would do anything for anyone else."

He nodded. "I'm sorry. I had to help Pinch."

"No need to apologize." She smiled at him, but her eyes looked sad. "Few get the best of that fairy witch. But it gladdened my heart to see the two of you coming through my door. I was about to take off after the little one. And don't you worry about him. He'll heal. One thing you can count on is a fae keeping a promise. It's nigh to impossible for them to break a sacred vow. And if they do, I've heard the punishment is death. Now, tell me what you had to give in return."

"I have to help her find a toy. Well, a family heirloom. And she said that if I didn't help her, one day Pinch would have to do it."

"That must be what your father was doing, with that old riddling spell. He wouldn't tell me everything. I know it was from fear of putting me in the path of Morga's anger. I could sense that by the way he didn't answer my questions direct-like." Moggety wiped her hands on her apron. "I'd hoped that with Heldor's death Morga might have given up on any foolishness she had going on with him."

"She called him a *fool!*"

"There, there. That's of no never-mind. Her way of talking twists folks all higgledy-piggledy inside. Heldor was no fool. He was a man trying to protect his family, and his friends."

She slapped the table. "But since you've left, I've been trying to remember that finding riddle your da told me. I know there was more than just the bit written on your door. Let's see—"

William interrupted her. "I know the whole thing. Morga chanted it.

> *Whiter than snow is love's light atremble.*
> *Thirteen for Morga—scooped in a thimble.*
>
> *Redder than blood are flames that will brand.*
> *Thirteen for Morga—clutched in bare hand.*
>
> *Blacker than night is death's icy kindle.*
> *Thirteen for Morga—fixed on a spindle.*
>
> *A thimble of love.*
> *A handful of flame.*
> *A spindle of death.*
> *And I'll go whence I came.*

"That's the rest of it!" Moggety said. "I'm certain I wasn't much help to your father, what with him not telling me everything. But I do know about that spindle. If it's the same one, it's been in the witch's family for ages—an evil thing her great-great-great-grandmothers used to put curses on. The stories say it's been hidden for years. If you should find it, don't touch it! Death is sure to be on it." Moggety paused to pick up the orange kitten.

"Those other parts of the spell are a puzzle," she added. "I think Heldor was working on some of it when he last came to see me. There was something secretive about him at that visit. I could feel it. If I'd only known he was going to Cliven Rock, maybe I could have stopped him." She shook her head.

"He had that part all wrong!" William said. "At least, that's what Morga said. She said Da shouldn't have gone up to the cliff. She said something like it wasn't sunbeams from some place that was loved. It was . . ." He stopped and, feeling a little silly, continued, "*love's light*. But I don't know what that is. Do you?"

"Say that first part again."

"*Whiter than snow is love's light atremble. Thirteen for Morga—scooped in a thimble.*"

Moggety furrowed her brow. "Love light, hmmm. Love light might be a common name for a flower. Wait! Did you say *love* light or *love's* light?"

William thought for a moment. "Morga said *love's* light. I'm sure. But what difference does that make? Do you know of it?"

"It makes a great deal of difference! Every word must be considered when dealing with the fae folk. Let's see . . ." Moggety ran her fingers through the fur on the kitten's back. "True *love's* light can only come from a body in love. And yes," she said, nodding. "I *do* know of it. Oh, yes!"

William waited for her to finish while she seemed lost in her thoughts. Finally, she said, "When a body loves another, there's a kind of light that shines from the eyes. It's the purest, most honest light there is." She reached out and touched the chain around William's neck. "The man who gave me this had that light in his eyes when he looked at me."

William eagerly pulled up the chain and looked at the blue vial. "Does it have love's light in it?"

Moggety smiled. "No, I'm afraid not. Though it is very special to me. Tuck it back against your heart. Besides, my gut tells me this has to do with your mother. And your father once said something odd to me. I remember it now. At the time I thought he was just generally speaking about her. Now I'm not so sure."

William dropped the chain inside his shirt. "What did he say?"

"He said that Lirian was like the sun, alight with love."

Ma! He jumped off the bench. "Ma must have true love's light. Morga said it wasn't sunlight. And she said Ma was in the Old Forest, too. You were right about that. I'm going again."

Moggety caught him by the shoulder. "In the morn. It'll be dark soon. And this time, that young rascal will not escape me, even if I have to hobble him with my apron strings."

Then she added, "The puzzle is, why your father would have gone to Cliven Rock to collect sunlight if he'd already figured out that bit. He must have gone for another reason. Stumpifications! I wish I'd pestered him more on that last visit. He was hiding something from me; I just know it! He seemed as jittery as a water bug. Hmm . . . what was he hiding?"

chapter 16

Traveling down the trail again, William kept a keen eye out for any sign of Pinch, or Morga and her *pets*. By the time he got into the high pastures, he was fairly sure no one was following him.

As he got farther down the mountain, the trail became a muddy road. When the first passerby appeared and nodded at him, William lifted his cap, saying, "God speed you, sir!"

After crossing the bridge that spanned the Dightby, he turned toward the towpath. But there was one thing he wanted to do before he left the village behind. Near the outskirts was the burying ground. He entered and stepped around the grave markers. At the base of a tree was a trampled area, with fresh clods of dirt at the surface. There, a simple piece of rough wood read: HELDOR, A FRIEND.

William bowed his head. A long time later, he swiped at his eyes and made his way back to the river. Da had died before he could bring Ma home. Now it was up to him to do it.

Walking along the towpath, he turned the tasks over in his mind. *Whiter than snow is love's light atremble. Thirteen for Morga—scooped in a thimble.* He scratched his head. "I wonder if I have to do the tasks in the order she gave them." he said aloud. He sighed. "No telling what might make it not work. I'd better whittle a thimble tonight."

A couple of times, William looked back at Crag Angorm. He could just make out a glint of silver that must be the river tumbling down. Pinch and Moggety were up there, so far away. And hidden in the white clouds at the peak was his home.

At first, he passed a number of people and animals on the path. And there were small boats on the river. Sometimes, when a boat passed, he waved. He wasn't sure how a person actually talked to an oarsman out in the middle of the river. How was he going to get a ride?

Over the course of the next two days, he passed fewer people. And on the third day, he didn't see a single boat. He stared back at Crag Angorm and stretched his hand out. The mountain seemed small enough to sit upon his arm. It made him feel as if his heart, too, was shrinking. He'd never been this far from home.

He sat down to rest. His feet hurt and the soles of his boots were wearing thin. If he didn't find another way to the Old Forest, he'd end up walking barefoot.

Whinnee . . . Aw-ah-aw!

"Aii!" William jumped up. What was that? He twirled around. No one was on the path. And then there was a snort, and another sound that was neither a bray nor a whinny. *Aw-ah-aw!* The sound came from a thicket of young willows on the river's edge.

William started down the riverbank. "Hello?" The thicket shook. He stopped and slowly pushed aside several willow saplings. "Oh!" It was a mule, mud-splattered and caught on the willow brush by a trailing piece of rope. On her rump was a raw gash.

"What are you doing here?"

The mule flared her large nostrils and rolled her eyes. William took a step back.

The mule nickered at him.

"Did you run off?"

Whinnee . . . Aw-ah-aw!

Her loud bray made him jump again. But he was used to working with animals. Sometimes he'd had to help Da rescue a goat. He approached her again, speaking softly. "There, girl, I'll get you free. Just—just hold still."

He pushed a sapling aside and found the end of her rope. It took him a few minutes to unwind the rope from around several of the willows until it was freed up. "Come on. Let's get a look at you."

He tugged the rope, and the mule stepped free of the thicket. She shook her head.

"There, now!" William backed up, unsure about how tame she was. She looked as if she'd been living off the land for some time. Staying clear of her hooves, he sidled around and inspected the wound on her rump. It wasn't bleeding, but it looked dirty. "Come on. Over here. Let me wash that sore spot for you."

The mule rolled her lips back and showed him her yellow teeth. But she followed him to the water's edge, where he lifted several cool handfuls of water up and over her injured rump.

"I'm headed to the Old Forest," he told her as he tended her. "You're welcome to come with me, if you want."

She shook her head.

"Are you hungry? There's some nice new grass coming up along the towpath." He turned her from the water and tugged at her rope. But she refused to move farther than the willow twigs, which she began to strip and chew.

William put his hands on his hips. It would be a relief to his aching feet if he could ride her. But she didn't seem interested in going anywhere.

He needed to get going. He couldn't wait around for the mule, and he wasn't sure if she'd even let him ride her. He bit his lip. Maybe he should cut the rope off her, at least. Then she wouldn't get caught up by it again.

He pulled Da's knife out and approached the mule. "Let me get my knife under the rope, and I can get it off you." As he slipped one hand under the rope around her neck, she yanked her head back. "Shh—shh, it's fine, girl."

He started to cut the rope and realized that he could slip it over her head instead. So he did, and tucked it into his bedroll. "Well, are you of a mind to come with me, or not?" he asked her.

She shook her head and continued munching on the willows.

"I guess not." William sighed and turned back to the path. The day was wasting away. He concentrated on putting one foot before the other. Soon the path led away from the river and toward a dense wood—the Old Forest.

William had heard tales of the Old Forest, and Moggety had said strange things went on there. Nervously, he readjusted his bedroll on his back and did not notice that someone was following him.

chapter 17

William stumbled onward. He'd been walking for three days. He was so, so tired. He dragged his bedroll along the ground. One moment he was staring at the sky, and the next moment he was looking at the ground. He fell onto the path—asleep. That is, until he was jostled.

"Pinch, stop that! What're you doing?"

Whinnee . . . Aw-ah-aw!

"Ahh!" William leapt to his feet. He promptly fell down again.

The mule's face was barely a hand's length from him. She laid one ear back and snorted.

"Oh, yuck!" William jerked just in time to avoid flying mule snot. "Why'd you do that?" He lay looking up the mule's nose before staggering to his feet.

He was about to turn from her in case she snorted again, when the ground went rushing dizzily away from him. He grabbed on to the mule's short mane and held himself upright. Then he closed his eyes and leaned into her shoulder. She was warm.

It took him a little while to realize that she didn't seem to mind him. Finally, he gave her an absent-minded pat on the shoulder and stepped away. "It seems you *are* going my way. That's good."

The mule nickered and started slowly along the path.

"Wait," William called. He picked up his bedroll and followed her.

They were only a short way into the Old Forest when the mule stopped at an upturned root ball. She turned her head to him.

He caught up to her and rested against her side. "What is it?" He looked at the mass of dirt and roots. Was there something there he was supposed to see?

Whinnee . . . Aw-ah-aw!

William jumped and took a couple of quick steps up the root ball. Was she going to kick him?

No. The mule pressed her side up against the roots and simply stood there. William thought he'd never understand mules!

He sat down on the root ball. His stomach growled. He'd have to find a place to rest and eat soon, though he hadn't much food left. But the mule wasn't moving. He looked for another way down and saw her broad back. Finally, he understood! She was offering him a ride.

He eased himself outward from the root ball and slipped his legs around the mule. Then he took her rope and slipped the loop back over her head. She didn't complain or try to knock him off. He put his bedroll behind him. Then he yawned and promptly slumped against her neck.

William dozed, off and on, and let his companion lead him through the Old Forest. He had no idea about which paths to take, anyway. And Moggety hadn't been sure of the way. So as long as they went deeper into the dark wood, he was satisfied. Tomorrow, when he had more energy, he would keep his eyes open for any signs of his mother.

They bedded down and spent a restless night at the base of an ancient oak. His dreams were full of throaty whisperings, as though the trees were gossiping all around him.

At daybreak they set off again. Every now and then, William noticed a green-tipped bud on the bare trees. The wood was coming back to life from its winter sleep. But even without leaves the forest was dim, for the tree trunks grew so close together they almost eclipsed the daylight.

They kept a steady pace and by midday came to a ridge. The path wound past a spring that leaked from the hillside. As William slid off the mule's back to refill his goatskin with water, he gave her neck a hug. He'd never have made it this far without her.

Then he scrambled higher to see what lay on the other side of the ridge. *Odd.* There seemed to be more sunlight here—in the middle of the Old Forest?

Book II

What is not known about the old tale is that the first princess never did prick her finger. The curse-laden spindle had its crown jewel plucked from it.

Then it was hidden.

Oh, yes.

It was hidden by twelve good fairies, sisters to an evil fae witch—the thirteenth daughter of a thirteenth daughter.

Until one day . . .

chapter 18

Beyond lay a glade. But blocking William's view into the center of the clearing was a tall, tangled hedge. It rose as high as some of the trees.

That was unusual enough, but what was truly strange was that the whole place pulsed with a golden glow. And there was a softness to it that lifted William's heart.

Quickly, William got the mule over the ridge. Then they rode the perimeter of the clearing. The hedge was made of thorns longer than William's hand. Morga had said his mother was in a safe place, behind a barrier. Well, this certainly seemed to be that! And the longer he spent bathed in the light of the glade, the more certain he became that his mother was there, beyond the wall of thorns.

The witch said he'd have to find the way through. But

he'd not found a passage in, though he'd often stopped and groped about in the tangles until his hands were torn and bleeding. Still, there had to be a way. Or else, how could his mother be within? And he knew, in the deep and tender places of his heart, that she was here. For although there was something sad about the light, it soothed his tiredness and cradled him gently.

Oh! To get this close and be stopped. He could barely stand it.

William walked up to the thicket and punched it. It was a useless gesture, but it made him feel better—except that the thorns tore another gash on the back of his hand. He idly rubbed at the cut. Then he leaned in, placing his head gingerly against one of the larger branches. A tear fell. It landed in a splatter of his blood on one of the thorns.

The wind quickened and sighed around him. William felt the hedge shudder. He tripped, backing away. The thorn thicket had seemed to suddenly come alive!

He steadied himself and saw it. A tunnel had opened into the base, right below where he stood. The pounding of his heart abruptly increased to a roar in his ears. He glanced to either side and then forced himself to turn and look behind him. Except for the mule, he was alone.

He took a few deep breaths. "I'll be back shortly," he told the mule. "Don't worry."

Then he got down on his hands and knees. The tunnel

was low, and narrow. He lay on his side and pulled at the hedge to inch into it. The thorns scratched his face. Bits of dirt and bark dropped into his mouth. And his hair got caught in the twisted growth.

At times, the tunnel was so tight he could feel the weight of the hedge pressing upon him. But there was no going backward. He couldn't have pushed himself feet-first back through, and he certainly did not have room to turn around.

Finally, it grew lighter in the tunnel. The weight of the hedge above him was lessening, and there was more air to breathe. He stretched out his arm and felt a breeze skip across the back of his hand. He thrust his shoulders and head clear. Stiff and tired, he pushed against the ground and dragged himself out.

William expected to find a tower or a castle inside the hedge, but there was only one low, slenderly arched building. It reminded William of the fancy lady's handkerchief his mother kept in a special box. Only, this one was pinched in the middle and set daintily upon four pointed tips. William gaped—he'd never seen anything so exquisite.

The two sides visible to him were open arches. And the light coming from the building didn't just shine out through the archways—the entire building shimmered. It looked like a glowing jewel upon graceful points, with its center pulled heavenward. Embroidered about its swooping arches were curlicues of green ivy.

But it looked deserted. William's hopes sank. He dragged his eyes from the tiny gemlike building to glance around the enclosure. The land inside the hedge was slightly rolling. All that it contained was the dry remains of what had once been grass. The only living thing was the ivy that scrolled around the arched entrances of the small structure.

As he came closer to the building, he could see through the nearest arch onto the dead field beyond. So there were arches on at least three sides. William wondered if there was a room off the fourth side. Probably there was another arch on the side he could not see, for the building seemed too small to hold a second room. It looked only large enough to keep five or six people out of the weather.

That thought no sooner entered his head than he felt a raindrop. "Bother!" The next moment, he heard the wind chittering as it crossed the hollow shafts of dead grass. That was followed by the plipping of more raindrops.

He raced to the single step that led up to the entrance closest to him. The top of the arch was low. He lifted the trailing ivy and tilted his head to pass under. Once through, he stood erect, for the ceiling rose as it followed the lines of the pointed roof.

He turned toward the hidden fourth wall—and quickly raised an arm to shield his eyes. He tried squinting through his fingers. The golden glow burned so intensely that when he shut his eyes he saw patches of blurred-out grayness.

William turned his back to the light and opened his eyes. He saw only fuzzy gray circles. He closed his eyes, then opened them. As his eyesight began to clear, he saw him—squatting against the inner wall of one of the slender arches. It was a gnome of a man, smaller than Pinch.

chapter 19

He was dirty, and clothed only in a

pair of breeches that looked to be held together by multiple layers of patches.

William rubbed his eyes. How marvelously red was the old man's beard! It shone like a crimson beacon out of the litter-covered pile of rags, and the baldness that made up the rest of the person. And how blue his eyes!

William closed his eyes again. Was he imagining him?

"Don't like what you see, heh?" The voice sounded low and gravelly.

"No," William answered as he quickly reopened his eyes, and then just as quickly closed them. "I mean—"

"Brash one, ain't you?"

William squinted past his lashes. "Excuse me?"

The little man leaned toward a dented metal bucket by his side and grandly spit into it. " 'Brash one!' I said."

"I'm not." William had been taught to be respectful to others, but for some reason this fellow made him want to snap. He hadn't even given William time to introduce himself.

Before William could say anything more, the fellow piped up, "And don't mind them owly circles you see dancing by. They'll pass in a mite if you don't take another peek at the light. Surprised you made it this far, scrawny, scratched-up bit that you be."

William looked down at himself. He was scratched all over from the hedge, but he wasn't scrawny!

Suddenly, the fellow yelled, "And stop that!"

"Stop what?" William asked as the rain abruptly

ceased. "Pardon me, but who *are* you?" He was too be-wildered to be polite.

"Welladay! And where's your manners? Asking me my name without so much as a *by-your-leave* from you?" The man waved his hand in a grand manner and spit again.

William took a deep breath. "I'm sorry. You surprised me. I didn't mean—"

"Surprised you, did I? I'll surprise you if I get my hands on you!"

"Wh-a-a—?"

"Be you dumb now, too—can't speak? Blinded and dumb!" The fellow shook his head.

William threw his hands up. "I'm not blind, and I can speak very well!"

"Ooh . . . think you're a big man, do you? Come to the Old Forest to threaten Tuli. I'm quivering with fear, I am." Tuli flapped his thin arms.

William opened his eyes wide enough to roll them in exasperation. He hadn't gone to all this trouble just to argue with a half-crazy old man. He still had to look for his mother. He took a sidling step toward the light with his eyes partially closed and his hand raised to his brow. All he could make out was that there was no arch on the fourth side.

"Ho, there!" the small fellow said. "One more step and I'll have to flatten your rude behind." Then from somewhere alongside him, he produced a cudgel. It was longer than William's arm and looked heavy at its two rounded ends. At the midpoint, where the man gripped it, the wood was carved away. He flailed it at William. "I can hit a fly at a dozen paces. So don't try it, you cutpurse!"

"Cutpurse! I'm not a thief!"

"Got your attention, *Mr. Too-Good-to-Tell-Tuli-His-Name*, don't I? Who else but a thief wouldn't give his name?"

William sighed, and then it came to him that perhaps this Tuli was another barrier—something like the hedge. Perhaps it was a matter of simply getting past him. He took a long look at Tuli and said, "Good day to you, sir! I am William, Heldor's son."

"That's better," said Tuli. "Pleased to meet you, William, son of Heldor."

William bowed his head in acknowledgment. "Pleased to meet you, Master Tuli . . ."

"A son of the Yana," Tuli finished for him.

William didn't know what, or who, the Yana were. Still, he responded, "Pleased to meet you, Tuli, a son of the Yana." Then he asked, "Why can't I approach the light? I believe . . . I *believed*"—he stressed the word, feeling not so sure of it now—"that my mother is here. I've been seeking her a long time."

Tuli eyed him thoughtfully. "You seek your mother?"

He placed the cudgel across his lap and stroked it. When he spoke again, it was to say, almost wistfully, "Had me a mother, once. She gave me this." He raised his cudgel—this time as though he was showing it off.

"She gave you *that*?" William asked, unable to keep the surprise out of his voice.

"And what's wrong with this? It's a fine thing. I could knock your head off with it. I doubt you've got anything so fine from your mother. I—"

William raised a hand and chimed in, "It's very handsome!"

Tuli lowered his face. "She left me when I were but"—he fumbled with his fingers and held up four—"two days old."

Two or four, William wasn't sure what the fellow meant. But that was awfully young to lose a mother. "That's terrible!"

Tuli seemed lost in his thoughts. After a moment, he roused himself and patted his pockets. "Ah!" He dug into a particularly filthy place and came up with a handful of rags. Slowly, he unfolded it.

William leaned forward and caught his breath. Tuli held a large gem of the purest green color. "What kind of jewel is it?"

"Don't know. But it's pretty, ain't it?"

"Yes." In fact, the watery green depths seemed to pull William in, closer and closer.

"My da gave it to me before he left."

William wrenched his eyes from the stone. "Your father left you, too?"

"Aye. When I were but twentyteen days old."

"What?"

"Aye. It was hard for the first while, with no da or ma. But I knew what the club was for. I got real good at using it. I could feed and do for myself." Tuli pulled a rag from one of his pockets and honked as he blew his nose. He wiped his eyes with the back of his hand and hiccupped discreetly. "But I don't know what this pretty stone's for what Da gave me. I'm hoping to have it figured out by the time I have three summers."

"Three summers!" William leaned back abruptly and peered hard at Tuli's wrinkled body and his head with its few wisps of white hair. "How old *are* you?"

Tuli stroked the green jewel. He hummed a little as he rewrapped it and tucked it away. After a moment, the fellow mumbled, "Old enough to do my job." Then, more loudly, he said, "So don't go sneaking any closer to the light!"

There was something in the grudging way Tuli answered that made William draw in his breath. Tuli was young! Despite the way he looked, he might even be younger than Pinch.

William had no notion about what kind of person, or Yana, Tuli was, but he had to get a closer look at the light coming from the far side of the room. He squatted down. "Tuli," he wheedled, "if you'll let me get close to the light, I'll play a game with you."

"Can't get close—it'll burn your eyes," replied Tuli, adding quickly, "What sort of game? Can I use my club?"

William hadn't thought this far ahead. "A—a guessing game," he said, thinking that might be safer than one with Tuli's cudgel.

Tuli considered this. "I like riddles." Then, suddenly, he slammed his cudgel against the stone floor, raising clouds of dust.

William rocked back on his heels, out of harm's way, and sneezed. *Now what?*

"Squarmy!" Tuli yelped, flailing about and almost smashing his spit bucket.

William saw a wisp of movement on the wall above the small fellow's head—a fast-moving yellow blur. Tuli twisted around and swung at it.

"What's that?"

"A bit of devilment, that be! Where'd the rogue get to?"

William pointed to the wall. "Up there somewhere."

"Squarmy! I'm going to tie your tail in knots!" Tuli swung his club up over his head and slammed it recklessly into the wall. Dust rained down on Tuli's head and shoulders. Then the fellow pursed his lips and gave a short high whistle. *Cher-ick!* "Get back here!"

William blinked. He thought he saw something leap through the air and land in Tuli's beard. Then it wiggled out of sight!

Tuli was quieter now. "He's nothing but a botherment. Caught him once trying to make off with my da's green stone. And it bigger'n him!"

"What is it?" William asked. "I mean, who . . . Or—"

Tuli cupped his hand over a spot on his beard. "Squarmy, say hello to our guest."

A tiny delicate snout topped by two perfectly round eyes the size of pinpricks blinked at William from Tuli's beard. The creature was as small as a grasshopper. Was it some sort of insect? William could well believe there might be vermin living on the fellow. He leaned in to get a better look.

"Impossible!" William whispered. And then, catching a whiff of Tuli's breath, he reared back. He pointed to the minuscule muzzle, which was now being cleaned with a faint spark of red tongue. "It looks like a tiny dragon!"

chapter 20

"**O**f course it is!" spluttered Tuli. "Humph! It's a right proper companion for a guardian. It seems to me you've a lot to learn."

The little man—for though he was young, William couldn't think of him other than as a man—leaned forward and asked, "And how old do *you* be, William, Heldor's son?"

William could not take his eyes off Tuli's beard. "I've got twelve summers."

"Never!" yelped Tuli. "And you no better educated than to not know a dragon when you see one." Tuli tugged at his beard. "Now, I heard once about . . ."

William barely heard anything Tuli was saying. He'd never imagined . . . a dragon! Hadn't the dragons died out in the misty ages? That was what all the stories said.

And guardians? Tuli had said he was a guardian. Moggety was the guardian at the falls. Her pets were not that unusual. William put his hand to his forehead. There was so much he didn't know about the world beyond Crag Angorm. But . . . dragons? "I thought the dragons were all dead," he said.

"Hush!" Tuli glared at him, putting a hand protectively over his beard. "We don't talk about such things."

"I'm sorry. It—he just surprised me."

The little fellow leaned forward and whispered, "He be the only one I know of. It's a sad story."

William nodded. He knew his mouth must be flopping open, but he just couldn't quite grasp the idea of a miniature dragon.

"*Arrgh!*" Tuli cleared his throat. "Now, don't be losing hold of that idea about a game. I like games. And even if you be a bit ancient for playing games, I can indulge you."

"Me? But I'm not . . ." William stopped. He reminded himself that Tuli was young. And in Tuli's eyes, he was old. As strange as this thought was, it wasn't as strange as knowing there were still dragons in the world. William nodded, more to himself than to Tuli.

The dragon was almost unimaginably mysterious, but William had to see what was in the center of that bright light. And to do that, he needed to get past Tuli. "Yes!" he finally said. "We can play a game."

"And what does the winner get?" Tuli rubbed his hands together.

"The winner gets to do one thing he desperately needs to do."

"Well . . ." Tuli considered. "How'll that work? Suppose I desperately need to fly? I can't fly. I'm not sure that'll work."

William wanted to roll his eyes. Instead, he said, "All right, the winner gets to do one thing he desperately needs to do that is physically possible."

"Provided it doesn't kill him," Tuli piped up.

"Of course!" William snapped, wondering if he was ever going to get a chance to take a good look into the light. "Have we got it? The winner gets to do one thing he desperately needs to do that is physically possible provided it doesn't kill him!"

Tuli scratched his beard. "I'm not sure. . . . Supposing you need to desperately get your hands on Squarmy? Or maybe you want my cudgel, or my da's green stone?"

William sighed and raised a hand. "I pledge that I will not take Squarmy"—though that was an exciting thought!—"nor your green stone, nor your cudgel."

Tuli slammed his club on the floor, raising another cloud of dust. "Aye! Let's do it!" Then he dropped his club, spit in one of his hands and held it out to William. "It's a deal!"

William coughed and looked at the spit-soaked hand.

He squirmed, but he spit in his own and clasped hands with Tuli. "A deal!"

"Who goes first?" asked Tuli.

"You," said William. For in truth, he had no idea about what sort of riddle he'd ask. He wanted time to think of one. And he needed to win the game—to look into the light.

"Aye, well . . ." Tuli scratched his beard. Squarmy peeked out as he did so. After a bit, Tuli asked, "What do guardians drink?"

"What do guardians drink?" William repeated. *Hmm* . . . Did they drink something that regular folks did not? What did Moggety drink? What did anyone drink? Cider? Ahh . . . tea. But what kind of tea? William had it. "Securi-tea!"

"Ugh!" Tuli roared. "You got it, right fairly. Now, one for me to puzzle at. Make it a good one!"

William licked his lips. Da used to love riddles. What was one of his hardest? "All right," he began. "What's white and covered with snow . . ." William paused. "No, wait! I have a different one. He leaned closer to Tuli and said, "*Whiter than snow is love's light atremble. Thirteen for Morga—scooped in a thimble. How do I get it for Morga?*"

Tuli's face went red. "Morga!" he growled. Then he turned and spit into his bucket. "You scoundrel! You never mentioned her in our deal! I ought to—" He picked up his cudgel and waved it. "I don't want no business with her. And that ain't rightly a riddle, nohow."

William tried to calm the fellow. "I know it's not. I'm sorry. I dislike her, too. But it's a puzzle I have to work out, a task I have to do to be reunited with my mother. I was hoping you could help me, that's all."

Tuli lowered his club. "Why didn't you say so in the first place? Aside from being a riddle-cheat, are you the one I've been waiting for?"

"Which one?"

"The one that'll wake my lady what I've been guarding all this time."

"My mother?" William rose and started to look behind him, but the light hit his eyes again. He threw his hands over his face.

"Don't know that she's your ma," said Tuli. "But the light, it comes from my lady. She cries and her teardrops glow so much, they're like tiny stars. They keep the whole place lit up so's a body can't hardly sleep around here."

"How can I see if it's her?"

"That's a real puzzle." Tuli whistled for the dragon. *Cher-ick!*

"What d'you think, Squarmy?" Tuli asked his tiny companion. "Is this William, son of Heldor, the one we've been waiting for? We thought the one we'd been waiting for was the tall fellow what came a few times.

When he got close and spoke to her, she stopped shedding her golden tears."

"My da!" William said. "I bet it was him. Only, he . . ." William dropped his head. "He fell from the mountain and died."

When William could look at Tuli again, he saw that both the little man and the dragon were weeping. The dragon's tears were so tiny, they were only sparkles on his muzzle. Tuli's were fat dollops of water.

"It's . . ." William was unable to finish his sentence. Finally, he said, "He was trying to find Ma and bring her home. Now I'm doing it. And I need your help."

Tuli retrieved the soiled rag he'd blown his nose on earlier. *Honk! Sniff, sniff!* "Squarmy and I'll help you. Here." Tuli pulled out yet another rag and held it up for William. "Tie this about your eyes."

William gingerly took it, hoping it hadn't been used for other things. He tied it around his head, covering his eyes. "Now what?"

"Hold out your hand."

William did, and something fiery hot dropped onto his palm! He screamed and yanked the binding from his eyes. He stuffed his hand under an armpit. "What'd you do?" Then he ran through the nearest archway to a puddle left by the rain and swished his hand in it.

chapter 21

William shielded his eyes from the light and staggered back inside.

Tuli's eyes were wide. "Aggh! I did not mean to do you harm. I forgot Squarmy can be hot to the touch. He don't burn me."

"Squarmy burned me?"

"He can't help it. It's all that fire in his belly." Tuli rummaged in his beard. "Come out here and make your apologies to William."

Squarmy poked his head out. And in a yellow flash, he ran down Tuli's chest and legs and over the floor to William's side. He bobbed so fast, William could only see a blur.

William leaned over. "It's all right! You didn't mean to hurt me."

Tuli tugged at one of his large ears. "I was hoping Squarmy could guide you to her. He's better with directions than me, running across a hand side to side, forward and back. I never quite got me the hang of it. But I'll give it a try if you put the blindfold on again and do what I tell you."

William nodded. "Only, don't burn me this time!"

Once William had retied the rag around his eyes, Tuli began, "Now, turn just a little tad partway round. Nope. Too much. Go back. Are you even listening?"

"I'm trying!" William inched around a bit.

"That's better. Now, step forward some steps what aren't my-sized."

William paused. "What-sized steps, then? And how many?"

"Regular-sized. Regular number."

"What's regu—!" William bit his lip. "Can't you just take my hand and lead me?"

"Aye. I could, but my clothes be biggish on me just now, and I'm afraid I'll trip us both. There not be much room up there by her bed."

William sighed, ground his teeth together and shuffled forward until Tuli yelled, "Stop!"

"Now what?"

"Give a body a moment to get it all exact like!" Tuli snapped. "There be a step. You got to get up onto a kind of platform. Let's see . . . can you shuffle your feet along until you feel the step with your toes? You have got toes?"

"Yes, I've got toes!" William snapped. Then he asked, "Squarmy's not close by, is he? I don't want to step on him."

"You won't step on Squarmy. He's faster than a greased piglet at the fair."

That was true. Still, William didn't feel very confident about this. Very slowly, he scooted one foot forward and then the other, until his boot hit something hard. He had no idea what he was headed toward, but whatever it was, it was making him warmer. Not hot, in the way one's skin feels hot, but a deeper kind of warmth—a kind of warmth that's felt inside. It made his heart feel as if it was floating.

"That's it," Tuli said. "Now, the problem be, you have to step up there and not go knocking about. And once you get up there, you need to stretch your hand out and lift a glass lid, and see what happens."

"See what happens? You mean, you don't know? The light could still keep me from looking at her?"

"Well, ain't we got to try something? And she's stopped her tears afore, with the other one what visited. Can't hurt to try."

William gulped. Tuli was right about that. It couldn't hurt.

Slowly, William raised one foot. How high? He

dragged it upward until it slipped over the edge. Then he slid it forward and put it down. So far, so good. He shifted his weight and . . . lost his balance.

"Watch it, you clumsy creature!" Tuli yelled as William went cartwheeling sideways.

"Yow!" William grabbed and caught some sort of smooth bar. He crashed, amid the sound of breaking glass. He landed with his head flopped forward and his legs splayed out. Well, he'd been wrong when he thought it couldn't hurt to try. It *had* hurt! He rubbed his back.

He hoped he hadn't landed on Squarmy. And what had he shattered?

Strangest of all, where was the light? It was gone. The rag around his face had slipped, and he could see out of one eye. He was facing an archway, looking across the glade. The room was bathed in ordinary afternoon light.

He heard Tuli muttering, "Now you've done it! And me a guardian, all this time with nary a problem."

William lowered the rag mask and untied it. Shards of glass were scattered about. He pushed himself up. Glass crunched underfoot. He turned to see the destruction he'd wrought, and saw . . .

"Ma!"

William leapt onto the platform, where a carved crystal bed sat, and upon which his mother lay. He raised her by her shoulders and hugged her. She did not respond. "Ma?" He laid her back down.

"Is she dead?" William cried over his shoulder. No, she couldn't be. She was warm, she was breathing—but she was not awake. "Why won't she open her eyes?"

William touched her cheeks. They had a healthy glow. "Ma?" He put his face down close to her mouth. Yes, she was surely breathing. He laid his head against her chest. Her heart was beating fast and strong. "Ma!" William cried again as he gently shook her. And now he was crying so hard he had to stop to wipe his tears away.

"She's not deaf," said a soft voice by William's elbow.

William sniffed and looked down.

Tuli had come and was sitting on the edge of the platform. He had his cudgel upright on the floor and was balancing his chin on one end. He lifted his face. "She be your ma, then?"

"Yes."

"She'll not wake, no matter how much shaking you do," Tuli said. "I've sung to her. I've whistled. I've nudged her glass bed. Nothing seems to wake her. The tall one what was here couldn't do it, either."

"What's wrong with her?"

Tuli shrugged. "She's sleeping."

William swiped an arm across his nose and eyes. His mother had never looked so . . . so regal, so beautiful! She had on a blue dress of the richest cloth, and it was displayed along the length of the cushioned bed. Her red hair held a circlet of—he leaned in close to study it—small jewels! Where had she gotten these things? She had only ever dressed in rough woolens. Why was she dressed like a fine lady?

"She's *got* to wake up," William said. "I've come to take her home." He looked down at his mother. The last of her golden tears trembled on her cheeks. He touched one with the tip of his finger.

"Squarmy and I been waiting for the right one to come and wake her. The other one tried, several times. When he talked to her, her tears quit falling and the light stopped spilling out. And see, you done that, too. She's not crying anymore. Not once you got close enough and spoke to her. So Squarmy and me, we know she can hear. Whenever the tall one left, she'd start weeping again."

William knelt by the glass bed. "What . . ." He cleared his throat and started again. "How did this happen?"

"Ah . . . you see . . . well . . ." The small fellow hesitated.

"Tell me!"

"Sit down here on the step; it's not a hasty tale. I've a bit of it from Squarmy, and that part's hard to put in words. Let's see . . ." Tuli crossed his ancient-looking hands atop one end of his cudgel and began.

chapter 22

"**M**any years ago, our king and queen had their first and only child, a beautiful baby girl—" Tuli was interrupted by Squarmy, who came slipping out of his beard to rest by his ear.

William saw a small flame. For a moment, he wondered if Tuli's beard ever caught on fire.

"Oh," Tuli said, waving Squarmy away. "Squarmy reminded me that this was a time when dragons were big and could frighten humans to death with just a look. He's right proud of that, he is."

"Go on," William said.

"Well, something went wrong, and the queen of the dragons—"

A tiny flame shot out of Tuli's beard.

"Whose story is this?" Tuli shouted. Then he composed himself. "She was a really *huge* dragon. As I was about to say, our good Queen Eleanor and the dragon queen were cousins—"

"Wait!" William held up a hand. "How could the queen's cousin be a dragon?"

Tuli grumbled. "If the two of you are going to be interrupting me every which way, how am I ever going to tell this tale? Just know that these two were cousins. *Sworn* cousins, not cousins of the blood." He pounded one end of his cudgel on the floor. "Now, let me finish! The kingdom wanted to celebrate the birth of the new baby, and the dragons agreed to deliver all the invitations. But one invitation was lost during a—"

"Wait!" William cried again. "This is the story of Princess Bree and the Sleeping Curse."

Tuli nodded. "That's the one!"

"Everyone knows that story. The princess pricked her finger and slept until—"

"No." Tuli shook his head. "That part got all upsey-downsey. You see, the good fairy sisters hid the thing what the princess was to prick her finger on. So the royal bloodline has lived on unharmed. Until now."

"What does that have to do with my mother?"

Tuli turned his blue eyes to William. "My lady is our present king's child. She's the heir to the throne and the curse."

"Ha!" William snorted. "She's not! She's my mother."

"Can you not see that she be dressed as a princess?"

William rose and stared at his mother. She looked

serene and queenly. And those seemed to be real jewels in her hair. But his family was poor! It didn't make any sense. The only fancy things Ma owned were a lady's handkerchief and the locket she always wore. "We've lived all our lives up on Crag Angorm," he said. "And Da—"

This time, Tuli interrupted William. "And your da . . . well, it sounds to me like he didn't escape the anger of the thirteenth daughter. The one what did not get an invitation to the celebration—Morga."

What! William whirled around. Did Tuli think he was living in the past? "Morga can't be the same evil fairy that cursed the baby princess. That was ages ago."

"Aye, the same."

"That means she's . . . she's . . ."

"Countless summers old," Tuli finished for him. "And let me tell you, she was not happy to have her death curse changed to a sleeping one! It's made her right cantankerous."

"Still, I don't understand what—"

In a flash, Squarmy appeared. He raced down Tuli's cudgel, across the floor and up the side of William's mother's bed. Tiny flames flickered from his almost-invisible snout. He was bobbing up and down.

"What's he doing?" William asked.

"Squarmy is begging your pardon again."

"Why?"

"Because he failed in his duty, and he be ashamed."

"Don't fret, Squarmy!" William looked at Tuli. "What should I do?"

"There's naught you can do. He has to get it out. You see, the dragons were to protect the children of the royal family. For years every generation of the royal heirs was kept hidden, and protected by a dragon. When a new royal baby came into the world, an older heir could ascend the throne. That way, the king and queen's family could live on. But Squarmy says it's taken a toll on the dragons. They've used up more 'n' more of their powers, and they've gotten smaller."

Tuli shook his head. "I told you it be a sad story. You mentioned Crag Angorm. Be that where you lived?"

"Yes."

"Aye, then I know what befell. One day I sat down on Crag Angorm to take out my green stone and have a look at it. And who should jump into my pocket when I wasn't looking but that little rapscallion!" Tuli stopped to shake a finger at Squarmy. "You see, I caught him trying to make off with my stone—the thief. There's something about my green stone that dragons can't resist."

So many questions danced around in William's head; it took him some time to sort out everything Tuli had said. Then it hit him, and he yelped, "Wait! Wait. You're saying I'm a—" Suddenly, he laughed so hard his side hurt, and it took him a while to catch his breath.

Tuli scowled at him. "I don't see what's so funny."

"You—you can't be saying that my ma will be the queen one day. And I'm some sort of prince!"

"If you're the one we be waiting for. And I'm not so certain of that yet, what with your coming in here and crashing all about." Tuli folded his arms. "On top of which, why hasn't Morga just put an end to your scrawny self? If you're of the next generation, you're the next heir. The line stops with you, not her. That is, if your story be true and my lady's your mother."

Tuli stopped to thump his cudgel. He added, "By my way of thinking, it don't do Morga any good for my lady to be in a forever sleep while you be traipsing about. That ain't no way to end the royal line. That's what's got me all puzzle-walloped."

"Me? The next heir!" William choked back more laughter and hiccuped. When he could speak again, he asked, "Do I look like a prince?"

Tuli seemed to give this some serious thought. "Only if princes look like they've been dragged through mud and attacked by maddened imps."

"No. No, there must be something missing from your story." William hiccuped again. "And if I'm a prince," he said, "what about my little brother, Pinch? He'd be an heir, too."

Abruptly, William stopped laughing. Morga had threatened him by saying she would come for Pinch if he did not help her get her heirloom back. *Come for Pinch!* Not just to get her toy returned to her but, perhaps, to put an end to Princess Bree's bloodline. Maybe Tuli wasn't so crazy?

William craned his head around to study his mother. She certainly looked as if she was in a forever sleep. Had she pricked her finger on the thing that was meant for Princess Bree?

Next to him, Tuli was spluttering. Finally, the little fellow croaked, "You got a brother?"

"Yes! And Morga's said she'd come for him if I didn't

help her find something she'd lost. She gave me some sort of riddle, or spell, with tasks to try to figure out. And she said I could be reunited with my mother." William rose and paced before the platform. Could Tuli's story be true?

Tuli squared his shoulders and thumped his cudgel once more for good measure. "So that be two of you Squarmy ran out on!" Tuli turned his blue eyes in Squarmy's direction. "Apologies be only part of what must be righted, you little rascal. Get back here."

A yellow blur leapt from the glass bed and burrowed into Tuli's beard. Tuli patted his beard a bit and asked, "Did you have sudden storms up there on the crag, with rain and lightning and all?"

William nodded.

"See? That be Squarmy's doings. I can't seem to break him of his weather-dreaming. Sometimes he kicks his legs when he's storming something up, and it ties my beard in knots. That was him, what got it to rain just afore you showed up."

"Weather-dreaming?" William's mouth dropped open. "Squarmy can make weather?"

"Aye. He gets right playful with the weather when he naps. But he ain't all full of mischief and running off on folks. He did his job, till he caught sight of that green stone." Tuli stopped to spit into his spittoon.

"Now!" He put his cudgel across his knees. "If

Squarmy and I can help, we will. Can you say that riddle which wasn't a real riddle again? It's the key, I'm thinking, as to why my lady be like this, and not yourself a-lying there."

William didn't answer Tuli right away. He went to his mother's side. Could his mother hear him? "Ma," he whispered. "I've missed you." He hung his head. "I don't care if you're a princess or not. I'll figure this out, I promise! Don't worry, we'll be together again."

He turned to Tuli. "I didn't tell you all of it. There're three tasks and then Morga will leave. It goes like this:

Whiter than snow is love's light atremble.
Thirteen for Morga—scooped in a thimble.

Redder than blood are flames that will brand.
Thirteen for Morga—clutched in bare hand.

Blacker than night is death's icy kindle.
Thirteen for Morga—fixed on a spindle.

A thimble of love.
A handful of flame.
A spindle of death.
And I'll go whence I came.

chapter 23

"**S**o there are . . ." Tuli started to count his fingers. "Hmm, let's see—"

William interrupted. "Three tasks. And then, I think, Morga will get back some sort of toy or heirloom."

"Right! I was getting there," Tuli said. "I'm thinking that the toy she wants may be the spindle what Princess Bree was supposed to prick her finger on, but never did. And there be a spindle in that last task."

"I—I guess so," William said. "If that old story is true."

Tuli snorted. "Of course it's true! I can see your education be lacking. Now let's see, we usually start with number . . . ah, number—"

"Number one."

Tuli waggled a finger. "There's naught to be gained

by rushing round willy-walloped about these kinds of things."

Impatiently, William chewed at the inside of his lip to keep quiet. He hadn't been rushing around *willy-walloped*!

"Now, I'll give it a thumping whack of thinking," Tuli continued, and closed his eyes.

This was going to take some time.

While Tuli hummed, and every so often muttered the words *love's light,* William inspected the crystal bed his mother lay upon. He shifted bits of broken glass and peered under the bed.

Then he realized he was having a hard time seeing. The day was waning. It had been her tears that had flooded the glade and the dainty building with light. Now those tears were gone.

He heard Tuli say *love's light* again.

"Yes," William said, turning to the small fellow. "Moggety said it's the purest light there is and it shines from the eyes of someone who loves you."

Suddenly, Tuli's beard flared. Squarmy was glowing, and that gave William some light to see by.

What he saw was Tuli blustering, trying to get his next words out. "You know of Moggety, the guardian of the falls?"

"Yes. She's my friend."

"Well, see there!" Tuli slapped his knee.

"See what?"

"Not just anybody be friends with the likes of Moggety. The guardians be charged by the good fairy folk with taking care of many things, but especially the royal family. Did you not know that?"

"No-o-o. No one told me that."

"Well, there you have it."

"Have what?"

"Sure, you're a prince, I'm thinking."

Despite Tuli's certainty about William's royal blood, William was still convinced there'd been some sort of mistake. He certainly didn't feel like a prince. Princes didn't live on snowbound mountain peaks and eat dried-up turnips and soft apples.

"Prince or not," William said, "I still need to collect love's light. I even whittled a thimble on my way here. But how can I collect any light from my mother's eyes when they're closed?"

He was never going to figure this out. He slid down to the platform and slumped beside Tuli. His stomach growled. He didn't care. He held his chest close to his knees, afraid that if he didn't hold his heart in, it would break and fall away from him.

When he finally raised his head, Tuli asked, "You got any more friends I should know about?"

William shook his head. "I don't *think* so." Then he remembered the mule. "I rode through the Old Forest on a mule. She's outside the hedge. I think she'll wait until I return. Is she a guardian?"

Tuli thought for a moment. "Nay, not heard of a mule what be a guardian. Of course, I've not heard of a mule, either."

"Oh!" William nodded, and his stomach growled again. "Sorry. I haven't eaten in a while." He wondered what Tuli did for food.

Tuli rubbed his stomach. "With all this puzzling and whatnot today, I've clean forgotten my own manners! Squarmy and I get most of our victuals from the sky. I'm right handy with my cudgel. And he can light a fire for us to cook over." Tuli rose. "Now, don't go crashing into anything else whilst I get us some supper. It be hard enough to keep the place neated up the way I like it."

William opened his mouth. It wasn't entirely his fault that he'd crashed against the glass lid of his mother's bed. He was about to say so when Tuli disappeared through one of the archways.

Later, Tuli cooked them a nice grouse over an open fire. And once his stomach wasn't complaining anymore, William yawned as he made his way to his mother's side. He put a hand on her forehead. "Good night," he whispered. Then he kissed her.

William felt a jolt. Something was happening. His mother's breathing deepened. "Ma?" He glanced over his shoulder. "Something's happening, Tuli! Come quick!

Ma? Ma?" He took her by her shoulders and raised her a little. "She's smiling!" he yelled.

"You don't need to bellow! I've got my hearing." Tuli was by William's side. "Aye. My lady's not the same. What did you do?"

"I kissed her good night. That's all."

"She smiled when the other fellow was here, too. But she ain't waked yet. See? Her eyes are still closed. Can you do it again? Maybe there be something in a human's kiss what helps a body, and she needs a mite more of it."

William kissed her again.

She trembled; her smile broadened. Her eyelids fluttered. They opened and . . . closed.

"Do it once more," ordered Tuli. "Seven times lucky, they say."

William kissed her a third time.

Again, her eyelids fluttered open for a moment . . . and slammed shut. But there was something else. In that brief moment William thought he saw a flash, like love shining out of them. And before he could kiss her one more time, large silvery tears began to squeeze out from under her eyelids and wobble their way down her cheeks. The room glowed with soft white light. It wasn't like the golden tears—it wasn't sad, and it didn't blind him. It was a light that made him feel happy and loved.

"What lovely light," Tuli whispered.

chapter 24

Yes. **William agreed with Tuli. It was** a lovely light his mother's tears produced. He turned in a circle as the room filled with it. And then, "Love's light!" he shouted. "That's it!"

He searched his pockets. He found his mother's lock of hair, but where was the thimble?

"What you be dancing about for?" Tuli asked. "You got the itchies?"

"No! No! It's my thimble. I whittled it and put it in my pocket. But I can't seem to find it. It *has* to be here."

Had he dropped it? He raced around the room, looking for it. Then he remembered the crawl through the hedge. But the night was dark. He'd never find it out there. Could he quickly whittle another? What if the white tears stopped? He grabbed at his head and groaned.

"Let's not get all addled up," Tuli warned. "What's this thimble look like?"

"Like a thimble!" William shouted.

"How big is it?"

"It's as big as a thimble! A thimble is shaped like a tiny hat, or your spit bucket. It fits on the end of a finger. It's—" He stopped and stared at Tuli.

Tuli's beard was wiggling. William strode over to the small fellow and leaned in to have a good look. Squarmy's tail and rear end were poking out. As William watched, the dragon fell out and landed on Tuli's chest. Squarmy had the wooden thimble in his paws.

"Be that it?" asked Tuli, looking down.

"Yes!"

Tuli plucked the thimble from Squarmy and gave it to William. "He's got all sorts of things hidden in there. They be his treasures." Tuli picked up the dragon. "Are you thieving again?"

Squarmy ran yellow circles around Tuli's hand.

"It's not me you need to make up to. It's our friend, William." Tuli held his palm up. "I'm afraid Squarmy took a shine to your thimble. There's no telling what will catch a dragon's fancy. And as you can see, they're not strong in resisting a fancy." He looked Squarmy in the face. "Now you'll have to make amends again."

Squarmy started to bob.

"It's fine, Squarmy!" William said. "You returned it.

Perhaps I'll need a favor from you sometime, and you can make up for it."

"I'm reckoning he owes you more than one favor. He's got to learn the wrongness of thieving. Besides, his dragon hoard is getting right heavy to tote around." Then Tuli whistled. *Cher-ick!* And the dragon dove into Tuli's beard.

"He's ashamed," Tuli noted. "And he ought to be! Taking what's not his." Tuli tried to look down into his beard. He shouted, "Are you listening to me, Squarmy?" Then he whispered to William, "That's why I keep my green stone all bundled up."

"Well, I have the thimble. Now I can collect the love's light," William said as he leaned over the crystal bed. "Let's see . . ." He scratched his head. "The spell says *scooped in a thimble.* Maybe if I just . . ." William scooped the thimble through the white light. Then he peered into the thimble. It looked empty.

Tuli squinted at it, too. "Wasn't there something with a number in that first bit of the spell?"

"Oh! That's right. *Thirteen for Morga.* Maybe I have to scoop it thirteen times?" William swept the thimble through the white light above his mother twelve more times.

"Did you get your numbers all in the right order?" Tuli asked. "I could've helped, but Squarmy be rearranging his treasures. He got me itching, and I took my eye off of you."

"I think so, but it still looks empty."

"Aye," Tuli agreed. "But witches be tricky. Maybe what Morga wants be in there, only we can't see it."

"Maybe . . . ," William said. "Well, I guess I have to let Morga know I have it. Thanks, Tu—" He glanced down and the little fellow was gone. "Where . . . ?" He turned in a circle. "Well, it seems I must do this alone."

He wasn't quite sure how to call the witch, but he felt certain it required some formality. So he lifted the thimble and called, "*Whiter than snow is love's light atremble.* Come, Morga! I have thirteen scooped in a thimble."

"Yes!" a voice whispered. "I'll come. For a thimble of love. A handful of flame. A spindle of death . . ."

"And you'll go whence you came," William said. He could feel the skin across his neck and chest tightening as Morga stole into the room.

She put her fingertips together. "Did I say I'd go after I got my toy? I suppose it must be so. The basic parts of the spell are old. They're not of my own making, and there's no changing it."

William studied her. It was odd to think that she'd been the witch present at Princess Bree's naming day. Tonight her hair was white, and she had on a simple white gown beneath her cloak. Her long, kinked arms hung almost to the floor. And her leathery face was smiling at William in a way that made him feel all twisted up.

"I've got love's light scooped in a thimble."

"I have to congratulate you. Your wretched father did not do as well." She stretched out her hand to snatch the thimble, then yanked it back, hissing.

She had only touched his hands briefly, but tears of pain came to William's eyes.

"Set it down!" she shrieked.

William placed it carefully on the floor. Immediately, he clutched his hands up under his armpits. They were burning, though not as much as they had when he'd pushed her away from Pinch's side. Still, he bit his lip to keep from crying out.

As she lifted the thimble, she glanced around the room. "Humph! Nice place your mother's got here . . . for a thief." She put the thimble to her lips. "What's this? There's nothing in it." Morga threw the thimble on the floor. "You're just as useless as your father."

"Wha-at? I don't understand. I scooped thirteen times through the light."

"And did you abide by each part of the finding riddle? I think not." Morga turned and stepped to his mother's side.

"Don't touch her!"

"Don't worry about that," Morga said. She didn't touch his mother but spent some time searching around the bed and under it. She even sorted through the broken glass.

"What are you looking for?"

"I told you—she stole my heirloom."

"There's no toy here. And she's not a—"

Before he could finish, Morga said, "I don't see it." She tilted her head and said, "Well, it hasn't been a total waste of my time. You've invited me in, past the hedge. It isn't easy getting past a barrier placed by all twelve of my sisters. Even with an invitation, I had to slash my way through. Still, I can come and go as I please now. Thank you."

Invited her in? What? *Oh, no!* He squeezed his eyes shut. He'd done it again. Once more he hadn't taken the time to think it all through. How dim-witted he'd been, yet again.

"Oh, don't look so distressed. It smells of dragon vermin here. It stinks, almost as bad as that herb-woman's hovel. I certainly won't be making myself at home. Tuli and his filthy dragon, pah!" Then she snorted and took another look around before addressing William.

"When I return, you'd better have the right light." With that, she whirled, her dress forming a cloud in the center of the room. Her last words lingered long after she'd gone. "I don't suffer fools for long. There's always Pinch to do my bidding."

chapter 25

William blinked. He took a shaky breath and blinked again. Tuli was sitting by his spit bucket. William headed for the puddle outside, to cool his hands. When he returned, he said, "We got it wrong."

"Aye. I heard."

William stepped up to his mother's bed. Several plump white tears lay quivering upon her cheeks. He raised his face to the soft light that bathed the dainty room. Then he slid his hands back into his armpits. "I was so sure we had it right." He turned. "Where'd you go, anyway?"

"It's not good to be where she be. She makes Squarmy all jittery so's he's a ball of running this way 'n' that till he don't know what be his top side and what be his bottom side. So we strolled off a ways. Not far—I kept my ears open."

William hung his head. "There's another thing. I did something stupid. I invited her in. Now she can come here as she pleases. I wasn't thinking clearly."

Tuli clutched his cudgel against his chest. "Aii! I did warn you that she be a tricky one. Even with my puzzling powers, I didn't think of that."

William sat down by Tuli. He put his head in his hands. "I'm sorry."

"No matter. I got Squarmy, and he has a good nose for trouble when it be about. But what do you reckon we did wrong?"

"*Whiter than snow is love's light atremble. Thirteen for Morga—scooped in a thimble,*" William recited. "We had love's light, which is whiter than snow. We had thirteen scoops with a thimble."

"I'd say it's that trembly bit that's got us gob-winked," Tuli offered.

"Yes . . ." William looked over toward his mother. "But how do we make the light tremble?"

"Could we sneak up on it and scare it?"

"You can't scare light!"

"Who says? You ever try it?"

"Of course not." William rolled his eyes.

"Well, I say we try it. Can't hurt." Tuli crossed his arms and glared.

"The last time you said something couldn't hurt, it did."

"How was I to know you're so clumsy?"

"I'm not. I— Oh, never mind." William rose and found the thimble. "I think there's something we're missing. If we just scoop it like we did last time, there's still nothing in the thimble to make tremble."

William went to his mother's side. He gently laid a finger against her cheek. A white tear dropped upon it. The light from the small round droplet wavered as it rolled along his fingertip.

"Let me see that teardrop. Maybe I can puzzle out where we went wrong," Tuli said as he pulled himself up against the bed and tugged down on William's hand to lower it. "Can you get it to stop being so wibble-wobbly? My eyes don't whirl around like that."

Suddenly, William slapped the side of the bed. "Tuli, you're a wonder!"

"I am?"

"Yes, you are." William laughed.

He tipped the thimble and slid the white tear into it. Then he pressed the thimble against his mother's cheek. Another tear rolled in. "See? It's the shining teardrops, Tuli! That's two . . . ," William counted.

As the third tear slid downward, Tuli yelled, "Five!"

"Quiet. That's only three."

Another tear rolled . . . "Eleventeen!" Tuli crowed.

William jumped. The thimble fell on the bed and out poured the teardrops he'd collected. He groaned and put a

hand to his head. "Would you please—" But that was as far as he got before a yellow flash clamped itself across Tuli's mouth.

"Whaaaaaa-r-r-!" Tuli clawed at his face.

Squarmy hung on as Tuli, looking like a ball of rags, began to roll around the floor. Every so often, William caught a glimpse of a glaring blue eye, or a blur of yellow. He smiled. "Squarmy, you've more than repaid me for the theft of the thimble!" He turned back to his task, collecting the tears anew. "One . . ."

As the thirteenth drop of love's light fell into the thimble, the crashing and banging behind William stopped. Tuli called, "Come back here, you rude gutterpup! I'll teach you a thing or two." He swung his cudgel about.

"Tuli. Tuli!" William waved. "Don't hurt Squarmy! Stop!"

Tuli dropped his cudgel and wailed, "I was only trying to help. I never learnt my numbers. Hadn't a teacher, you see. Nor ma, or pa." He sniffed and swiped at his eyes. "And that rapscallion kept me from helping you."

"No, no! You helped. You do your puzzling out loud, while you're talking. And you made me think of the answer. I couldn't have done it without you. You're a good puzzler."

"I am that." Tuli sniffed once more. "About Squarmy, not to worry. Can't hurt that rascal, no ways. He's too fast for me, and he knows it!" He gave William a little smile, then whistled. *Cher-ick!* "Come here, you ornery besetment. I miss you."

There was a flicker of yellow as Squarmy jumped into Tuli's beard. Tuli patted his tangled red mat. "You going to call her again?"

William held the thimble up. "Yes."

Tuli and Squarmy slipped out into the night.

It made no difference, now, that William was standing in the tiny building when he called for Morga. The witch had said she could come and go as she pleased. But in preparation, he braced himself by planting his feet firmly and clasping the thimble with fingers from both hands. The last thing he wanted to do was to drop it. The tears had stopped, and there might not be more. He needed to get this right.

"*Whiter than snow is love's light atremble.* Come, Morga! I have thirteen scooped in a thimble."

She was still dressed in white, and scowled as she said, "Aren't you a busy bee? I do hope you've done it correctly. I get angry when someone wastes my time." She hissed as she smiled at him, showing her tiny sharp teeth. "And you don't want to see me angry."

William's heart raced. He raised the thimble. The light from the tears in it trembled as the glow overflowed the tiny wooden container and swirled about him. He could feel his heart settling down. He let the light caress his face. His mother's love was all he had to guide him in the dark. "I have it right."

Morga pointed to the floor, and William carefully set the thimble down.

She lifted it and raised it to her lips. With a scornful look at William, she tipped the thimble and swallowed the light.

chapter 26

The light was gone. William heard a groan. A moment later, he was almost overcome by the smell and feel of damp smoke. He grabbed at his throat, hacking.

A dim gray glow quivered near the floor. The fae witch had fallen. Her white gown was rippling with a sickly light that swirled across her gown like shadows flitting. Morga was writhing at his feet.

Watching her, William felt his stomach go queasy. She seemed to be in such pain. He stretched out a hand to her.

"Don't touch me!" Morga folded herself in half and attempted to rise. When she finally got upright, she brushed her hands shakily down her gown. "Well, that could have been worse." She took a step toward an archway and stopped.

"Ugh!" she declared. "What horrible-tasting stuff! But then, she wasn't a very good mother, was she? Leaving you like that. No wonder her love's light tastes so vile."

William's mouth dropped open.

Morga patted her white hair. "Well, you've finally got one task done. More than your father managed." She stepped out into the night. Her last words were thrown back at William. "One is done! Now, two's to do."

William slumped shakily against a wall. He wrapped his arms around himself.

He must have slept, because sometime later he jerked awake. *Whinnee . . . Aw-ah-aw!* "Huh?"

The sound came again. *Whinnee . . . Aw-ah-aw!*

William rubbed his eyes. There was a small fire burning near one wall where Tuli slept with his head on his cudgel. William struggled to his feet and ducked under the ivy to peer into the night. "Hello," he whispered, and almost bumped into the mule's muzzle. She stood with her front hoofs on the step. In her mouth hung his bedroll.

"Hah!" William laughed, taking the rolled pack from her. "How'd you get through the hedge?" He looked past her shoulder toward the thorny barrier, but it was too dark to see. Then he gave her a big hug and found he was still feeling shaky. He hid his face against her neck and breathed in the dusty smell of her.

The mule turned to snuffle at his ear. William didn't even mind her slobber. With his face pressed against her, he could—almost—be calm again.

Tuli's sleepy voice came from behind him. "That be a mule?" he asked, holding up a glowing Squarmy.

"Yes."

"Odd sort of creature, ain't it?"

"I don't think so." After meeting Morga, Tuli, and Squarmy, William liked knowing just a *plain* mule.

Whinnee . . . Aw-ah-aw!

"How'd she get inside the hedge?"

William shrugged as the mule brayed once more.

Whinnee . . . Aw-ah-aw!

"Be that her name—Whinny Aw-Ah-Aw?"

"No. I haven't thought of a name for her yet."

"You ain't?" Tuli said. "Seems like that's not real mannerly. Hard to talk with a body if you don't know what to call it. You oughta give her a right pretty one. How about Lorna-Belle? I once knowed a Yana named that. Your mule's yellow teeth done put me in mind of the color of her hair."

William raised an eyebrow at Tuli's suggestion. He still had no idea what a Yana was—what Tuli was—but he kind of liked the name. "Lorna-Belle," he repeated, and the mule nickered.

"See there!" Tuli said. "She likes it, too."

Whinnee . . . Aw-ah-aw!

"Now, can you see if Lorna-Belle will stop her cater-wauling so's a body can get some sleep around here?"

William chuckled. "Sorry she woke you. But I'm sure she'll settle down now. Won't you, girl?" He gave her a little push off the step. "You stay out there. I'll see you in the morning."

Then he spread out his blanket and lay down next to his mother's glass bed. "Good night, Tuli and Squarmy," he murmured. The last thing he did before falling into an exhausted sleep was to whisper "And good night, Lorna-Belle."

In the morning, William forced his eyes open and saw Lorna-Belle blocking one of the archways. She was eating the only green plant growing in the clearing—the ivy that decorated the building.

"You'd best stop that creature afore it starts munching at the walls, too! And then we'll have a pretty mess, what with my lady's lid broken," Tuli said.

William stretched and rose to stand by his mother. She was still sleeping, her face calm and beautiful. He kissed her good morning. He waited. Nothing happened. He pushed his fingers through his rumpled hair and turned to take care of Lorna-Belle.

He caught sight of Tuli. *What!*

Tuli was bigger! He'd grown during the night to half again as large as he'd been the day before. Now he was bigger than Pinch. He was almost William's size. William rubbed his eyes. "Tuli," he said, "you're bigger. Or—or am I just seeing things?"

"I hope you be seeing things. You got eyes!" Tuli retorted.

"But . . ." William pointed a finger. "But you've grown. Overnight!"

"Growing's part of living. Don't you wake up and be a different size sometimes?"

"No!" William said. "We—I—I mean, yes, we grow. But it's a little bit all the time until we get one size. We don't grow a *lot* bigger overnight."

"That sounds tiresome," Tuli said, "always creeping taller. I often wake up a different size. Thought you might, too. Maybe you got a bit of dragon in you? Squarmy's always a tiny rascal. It can be a right bother when I awaken closer to his size."

When Tuli was closer to Squarmy's size! Why then, all anyone would see of him would be his pile of rags. "You get—get—get smaller, too? How—"

"Stop that!" Tuli interrupted him and waved a hand toward the archway. Then, turning back to William, he said, "While you're jabbering at me, Lorna-Belle be stripping all my pretty vines away."

Oh, yes, the mule! William stepped out to greet her. "Good day, Lorna-Belle."

She stopped her munching to eye him. Then she yanked off another strip of ivy.

"Um, Lorna-Belle, do you think you could not eat the ivy? And let me see how your sore is doing." William got her to turn around. "It seems to be healing. Now, go eat something else."

Lorna-Belle twisted an ear and plodded off toward the hedge.

William followed her with his eyes and saw the thorn barrier. Where he had tunneled through the day before, there was now a gap that looked to have been hacked out of it. Morga's doing—he was sure. She'd said she'd had to slash her way in.

Then he rubbed his eyes again. There was something else about the hedge. It was shorter than it had been the day before. The hedge was shorter, and Tuli . . . Tuli was taller.

William went back inside. He looked at Tuli and blinked several times—just to be sure.

Tuli held up a piece of meat on a stick to William. "Done made you something to break your fast. Best get it eaten afore that fire-breathing thief sneaks up and makes off with the last piece."

William took it, still staring at his red-bearded friend. He couldn't quite get his thoughts all lined up. "Tuli, the hedge is shorter today."

"Aye. It does that. Put there by the fae folk to protect your mother."

"But—but why? I mean, how . . . and you?" He pointed at Tuli. "You've gone in the opposite direction, up."

Tuli nodded. "Aye. That be how it is with me. Sometimes I grow up, and sometimes I grow down. And the hedge grows, too, only in the opposite direction. Haven't reckoned out, yet, why the fae folk set it all to working that way. But it sort of keeps me company, what with my lady not being a big talker. You got nothing like that?"

"No."

"Well, you may have lived a long life already. But it were lacking in ways. You got no cudgel, you got no spit bucket, and nary a thing to help you figure out which way you be waking up of a morn." Tuli shook his head sadly. "But I've got my puzzling powers to help you. So that be in your favor." He rubbed his hands together. "Now, where were we?"

William shook his head to clear it. "We've got the second one to work on. *Redder than blood are flames that will brand. Thirteen for Morga—clutched in bare hand.*"

"That's the one," Tuli said. "I just need to have me a think, and we're sure to get it sorted out right quick."

William wasn't so certain about that. He'd already given the second task some thought. And while his mother could supply the love's light needed for the first task, how could she help him with fire?

chapter 27

No, ma couldn't help with this one, even though part of it seemed easy. A lot of fires glowed with red flames and would brand you with a scar. But how to hold them in a bare hand?

William went out into the sunshine. He studied the swooping valleys between his fingers and the fatty bulges at the base of his thumbs. His hands should be scarred, or at least red and swollen where Squarmy's and Morga's touch had burned him. They weren't. However, they did seem different. The skin looked thicker, as if it was callused. He supposed that was to be expected, what with all the rough living he'd been doing.

When William was finished studying his hands, he saw that Tuli had joined them outside. He asked, "Have you come up with anything?"

"Aye. I've put my powers to it, and what I figure is we need red flames and a bare hand."

William only just managed to stop himself from rolling his eyes. "Yes. That's *exactly* what we need."

"See, I told you I'd get it all sorted!" Then, more quietly, Tuli added, "And I got an idea about them flames. But I don't like mentioning it."

"Tell me. Anything you know might be helpful."

"Well, you see, when I was making my way past your mountain, I had the feeling that someone be calling me here to the Old Forest." Tuli looked over his shoulder toward the dark trees. In a hushed tone, he added, "This forest be an odd place, and old. Even older than the fae folk!"

William's eyes followed Tuli's. Beyond the hedge, mammoth trees stretched their limbs skyward. He'd not slept well the night he'd spent under a massive oak on his way here. And Moggety had warned him about the forest. "What are you saying?"

"I'm saying it be alive."

"Of course it is. The trees are growing."

"More than that. I mean there's a real heart at its center and it beats with . . . with a red fury. I seen it." Tuli gulped and ran inside, groping for his spit bucket. He flipped it upside down and stuck it over his head.

"What are you doing?"

"Forget I mentioned that," came Tuli's mumbled reply. "It's too . . ."

William lifted the spittoon from his friend's head. "Too what?"

"Too scary." Tuli covered his face with his hands. "I didn't like the place. I—I only brought it up because that heart was on fire. Red flames shooting out of the earth. I saw it. And there be an even stranger bit—none of them burned me at all. I thought it was the end of me and Squarmy. The little vexation ran right out to the lip of that bottomless pit, just a-frolicking. So I crawled out and stuffed the rascal back into my pocket. But not afore that roiling fire spit flames all over me and tried to drag me into it." Tuli's eyes were huge.

"It didn't burn you at all?"

Tuli lowered his hands and shook his head as William rose. "Not even a scorch mark."

William took a turn around the room. He looked at his mother, and then at Tuli. "So you're saying that, maybe, I could hold some of that fire in my hand and it wouldn't burn me?"

"I'm not sure if it'll burn a human. Now, if you was a Yana—"

"I'm not."

"No. But I don't hold it against you. Da always said to be kind to the simpler sorts. Anyway . . ."

"Hmm . . ." William paced some more, barely hearing Tuli. Until he stopped and asked, "What was that you said?"

"I was saying not to go to the heart of the Old Forest. There be something else scary about it."

"What?"

Tuli looked for a moment toward the trees. "It was like someone got into my head. And wasn't nothing I could do about it. Couldn't move till it was done with me."

"And?"

"And as soon as it let loose of me, I ran off with Squarmy. We came here, where I found that my lady needed me. And here we been ever since."

William nodded. "It sounds like I've got to go there. If I can find it and catch thirteen flames in my hand, the second task will be done."

Tuli dropped his head, and a teardrop raced down his cheek. "I don't know why I ever told you about it. What if it swallows you?"

"It won't. I won't let it."

"You promise?"

"I promise."

Tuli's lip quivered. "Good."

chapter 28

William and Lorna-Belle spent two
nights sleeping fitfully within the forest's embrace.
There were no beaten paths to follow. Instead, the mule
led them around moldering hummocks of fallen trees,
past spongy seeps that wept up onto the leaf-mold, and
through the dark slits between giant trees.

On the third day, William saw that the forest was
getting greener. It shouldn't be this leafy yet. And there
was something about this strange greenness that told
him he was headed in the right direction. He patted
Lorna-Belle. "Not much farther, I think."

A moment later, she halted and would not take another step. William touched her lightly between her
ears. "If you can't go any farther, that's all right. Wait
here for me, if you can. I'll head into the greenness. That
seems to be the way."

In fact, he was sure that was the way, because for some time he'd felt a tug at his thoughts and at his heart. It was pulling him forward. The pull quickened his breath. And it frightened him—the way high places sometimes did when he wondered what would happen if he leapt. A thought came unbidden—what would happen if he fed himself to the appetite of the Old Forest? He knew it wanted him.

It wanted him, *now*.

Lorna-Belle whinnied.

William's hands shook as he slid from her back. When he did, he grabbed blindly for anything to keep himself from standing up and rushing madly forward. And it was some time before he realized that he was crawling—crawling onward with his eyes closed. He'd lost track of Lorna-Belle. He'd lost track of time, why he was here and even who he was.

His whole being was empty but for the swell and ebb of the forest echoing the *whump-whoosh* of blood through his veins. It pounded in his ears. He was blind, deaf and numb to all else.

In a voice loosed upon the world before man, before fae, before there was a single green growing thing—yes, he knew it was such a voice—came the command: *Come to me!*

"I come." William stretched forward a hand.

He tumbled into emptiness and landed with a thud. He opened his eyes. He lay at the base of a ridge. Above, the forest had opened its arms to the blue sky. He smiled and rolled over. Within reach, a pool shimmered. Its waves lapped at the gray rock on which he lay.

You are thirsty.

Yes! I am, he thought.

Drink.

He pulled himself to the edge of the pool. He put his hand against his chest to keep his shirt out of the water, and a sudden chill made him shiver. Through the thin fabric he'd touched Moggety's vial. He pulled the chain from his shirt and held the vial. A woman appeared. Two kittens sat near her feet. He knew her. But . . . *but who?*

She threw green dust into the air. Then she put her hands on her hips. "Who are you?" she demanded.

He fixed his eyes on hers. Despite her fierce tone, she had a friendly face. "I'm . . ." Who *was* he? "I'm . . . I'm . . ." The word he wanted kept slipping away. "Pinch!"

"No." The woman shook her head. "You're Pinch's brother. What is *your* name?"

She was right. He wasn't Pinch. He bit his lip. *Think.* There was Pinch and . . . Pinch and . . . "William!"

"Ach, good! And where are you?"

He took his eyes from hers and blinked several times. He lay on a boulder that overhung a deep fissure. Red flames leapt just beyond his fingertips. There was no shimmering pool to quench his thirst.

"I'm—I'm at the heart of the Old Forest. To get . . ." He pointed to the fissure. *Strange.* There was no heat rising from it. He waved his hand above the flames. "I need to get thirteen flames in my hand." He looked up at her. "And you're Moggety. A—a sending, I think."

"Aye. You're working on that fae witch's second task."

"Now I remember. Thirteen flames for Morga, in my bare hand." He got to his knees. "Will this work?"

"That I do not know. But you'd best be about it in a twinkling." She raised her arms. "I've not a lot of power this far from the river. The Old Forest may be stalled for a wee bit, but not for long. 'Tis a powerful force which was here before any of us, and will be here long after we're no more. Now, do what you must. And I'll do what I can." With that, Moggety suddenly seemed to be buffeted about as though she stood in a fierce tunnel of wind. The kittens got to their feet and braced their paws—orange and gray fur ruffling.

William gulped and nodded at Moggety. Then he got to his knees and scooted close to the edge. There was no heat, but that did not mean there would be no pain. The fire had not burned Tuli, but William was not a Yana.

With one hand he held tightly to Moggety's vial. He took a deep breath and swiftly scooped his other hand through the flickering red flames. Then he clenched it.

He leaned back. It hadn't hurt. He opened his hand. Nothing. *Nothing?* That couldn't be right. He glanced at Moggety. Her wide face was set in a grimace as her clothing, hair and cap ballooned wildly in the wind.

Still gripping Moggety's vial, he got down on his belly. Then he took a deep breath and dropped his empty hand and arm down into the fissure. It did not burn. He

exhaled. Then he caught a handful of flame. Not raising his arm from the fissure, he opened his hand amid the leaping flames. His palm danced with fire. *Good.*

Twelve more times he grabbed at a handful of flame, hoping that each time the number of flames in his fist increased. It was impossible to tell for sure. With his arm dangling in the pit, he shouted, "I'm going to call for her!"

"Crumpelstilts! Do it right soon," the sending of Moggety cried. "I'm losing my hold."

He turned his face to the side. "*Redder than blood are flames that will brand.* Come, Morga! I have thirteen clutched in bare hand."

This time, the witch of the fae folk wore a gown of deep red, almost blood-colored. Her hair was copper-red, and she looked much younger than the last time William had seen her.

He said, "*A thimble of love. A handful of flame . . .*"

She waved his words away. "I know. I know. I'm supposed to go somewhere when all this is done." She studied him a moment and then rubbed her hands together. "Well, I never thought I'd say this about a human, but you do surprise me! Here you are"—she turned and glared at Moggety—"and that herb-woman, too. At the beating heart of the Old Forest. Not many make it here and live to tell the tale."

Then the witch turned to Moggety. "Hmm . . . Having

169

trouble there, old woman?" she asked, and yawned as she took her time returning her attention to William.

A wave of energy shot through William. "Leave her alone!"

Morga rushed at William and pulled herself up short at his side. "No one gives orders to Morga! Do you want your precious brother to be safe?"

Before William could stop himself, he raised his head and snapped, "Do you want your red flames, or not?"

A shudder passed through Morga, and she brushed her hands down her dress as though calming herself. "We have a pact." She sighed. "I'll take those flames and leave the herb-woman alone . . . for the moment." She knelt down. "Only, you mustn't touch me."

"I won't. But can you lean your head down into the pit, a bit?"

"Hah! You'd like that, wouldn't you? And then what, you'd push me in? No. Raise your hand quickly and maybe I can suck up the flames." Morga brushed back her hair. Then she leaned in toward William.

"Now!" he said, quickly lifting his hand.

She placed her mouth near his fist.

He opened his hand. It was empty. "Wha—"

Morga leapt to her feet. "You fools! The flames are gone, and the fire here isn't even hot enough to brand anyone. Don't toy with me, you'll regret it!" She grabbed at her red skirts with one hand and angrily stomped her foot on the rock. Then she whirled in a red, vicious rage until she'd disappeared.

William sat up and looked at his hand. While it was in the fire, he had held flames. But it was true—they weren't hot.

Moggety interrupted his thoughts. "Go! Away from the pit. I can't . . . I can't hold the forest back much longer. Quickly!"

William jumped to his feet. He hesitated as he passed her.

"Don't stop," the sending said. "I'm not really here. Run! As fast and as far as you can."

William scrambled up the steep ridge. At the top he sped off, not worrying about the way. His name was William. He was in the heart of the Old Forest. He must run. *Run! I'm William. I'm William . . .*

He ran until his legs gave out. He ran until the deep greenery gave way to the pale buds of early spring. He stopped. *I'm . . .* What was his name? There was a waver at the edge of his vision. Something hissed in his head. He put his hand on his heart to quiet the pounding of his chest. *Must think.* He touched Moggety's vial. "William," he mumbled. And then he stood straighter, took another step and shouted, "I'm William! I've been to the heart of the Old Forest and lived."

chapter 29

Something wet plopped on his cheek.
Another splat hit him on his nose. William cracked his
eyes open. All he could see was yellow teeth. They were
dripping slobber. *Whinnee . . . Aw-ah-aw!*

William shot up. "What! Oh . . . it's you, Lorna-
Belle." He wiped his face, trying to still his racing heart.
"You can stop slobbering on me now."

The mule shook her head and backed away.

He'd fallen on a shaggy mat of brown moss. "You
waited for me. Thank you."

He got to his feet and steadied himself against her.
He'd failed at the second task. There was nothing for it
but to return to the glade and try again.

A Pinch-sized Tuli welcomed them as they made their
way through the hedge. "You made it! You didn't fall

172

in," he called. "Did you do it? Did you get those flames for Morga?"

William slid from Lorna-Belle's back and patted her flank. Then he pushed her off toward a patch of grass that was greening up in the glade. "No. It didn't work. When I raised my fist from the pit, the flames disappeared."

He sat on a step. Tuli sat as well, and balanced his chin on his cudgel. When he did, Squarmy came out of Tuli's beard and sat on his shoulder.

William sighed.

Tuli gave a huge sigh.

Squarmy gave a tiny sigh, and out came a scarlet flicker of fire.

"Somehow I need red flames." William scratched his head.

"Aye." Tuli scratched his chest.

Squarmy scratched his belly and flared again.

Sometime later, as dusk was deepening, William was startled from his thoughts. "Did you see something move?"

"Just that squirrel that be whirly-gaggling all about," said Tuli.

"A squirrel?" William rose from the step and stretched. "Where . . . Aiii!" The squirrel raced beneath his mother's bed, over the step and across William's feet.

"Watch it!" William yelled. He completely lost his footing and slammed sideways. *Oh, no. I'll crush Tuli!*

Tuli was swift. By the time William was halfway down, Tuli had jumped out of the way. But Squarmy flew free of Tuli's shoulder and sailed through the air. William reached out and grabbed the little dragon before they both hit the ground. "Ow!" He scowled at the squirrel as it bounded across the glade. Then he rubbed his shoulder with his free hand.

William opened his other hand. "Are you all right, Squarmy?"

Squarmy wasn't moving. "Oh, no! Squarmy . . . Wake up!"

Tuli came over and pulled William's hand down. A fat teardrop landed on William's palm. "Squarmy, you old botherment. Don't scare Tuli. Here . . ." Tuli fumbled in his rags and found his green stone. "Have a nice long look, boy. Come on, Squarmy."

More teardrops were flooding William's hand, and he couldn't tell if all of them were Tuli's. He trembled. What had he done? Then he felt a tickle. "Squarmy?" *Please, please.*

It began to rain.

"Something's happening," William said. "He's moving."

"Squarmy, are you storm-dreaming again?" Tuli asked. "Now's no time to take a nap when we're all rattle-clenched about you."

There was a bang, and a dust cloud rose. William jumped.

Tuli had smashed his cudgel against the stone step. "You little gutter-pup, wake up!"

William coughed, covering his mouth with his left hand. And then it hit him. "Tuli," he murmured.

"What?"

"I'm holding Squarmy in my hand."

"I be looking at that bit of vexation right now! He's always taking weather-making naps when he shouldn't."

"But—but I'm holding him."

"I can see that. Has the fall addled your brains?"

"Tuli!"

"Aye!"

"I'm holding Squarmy."

"Aye!" Tuli screamed.

"And he's not burning me!"

"Aye!" Tuli started to slam his cudgel again, then stopped. "What?"

"He's hot, but he's not burning my hand. Look."

Squarmy, uncurled in William's palm, yawned at them. Out came a small red flame. William was holding a dragon! Pinch would never believe this. He could hardly believe it himself. Squarmy had been knocked about and squished a little, but it had only made the dragon sleepy.

While Tuli was giving Squarmy an angry piece of his mind, William was smiling. His palm did feel hot where Squarmy's belly touched his skin, but not painfully so.

He thought about his hands as the tiny dragon's minuscule red flames flared briefly in the dim evening light. Finally, he said, "Here." He handed Squarmy back to Tuli.

Then he laid his palms against his cheeks. His hands were leathery. He pushed up his sleeves and saw that his arms were a deep brown from all the time he'd spent in the sun. But that coloring stopped abruptly at his wrists. It didn't look natural. The only thing he'd done with his hands that was unusual was to touch Morga, twice. And, once, Squarmy had burned him. Had that been enough to build up some sort of thickened calluses?

And then he remembered the healing liquid Morga had splashed all over Pinch. At the time, it had soothed his burning hands. Had it done something else to them? He wasn't sure. But watching Tuli's beard light up as Squarmy snuggled himself into it, he suddenly had an idea.

chapter 30

Tuli did not like William's idea! For most of the next day he hid his head under his spit bucket. It wasn't until Squarmy had made a point of frantically bobbing around them that Tuli had finally given in and taken it off.

"What's he saying?" William asked.

Tuli shook his head. "I don't like it."

"What?"

"Squarmy says he'll give the witch his flames. He's ashamed of leaving you all alone on the crag, and not doing his job. My lady might not even be here but for Squarmy leaving. He'd like to make amends."

William peered at Squarmy. "Are you sure you want to do it?"

Squarmy ran up to perch by Tuli's ear.

"He says only if we'll put a rag over his eyes, like you wore when you approached the light. He doesn't want to see the witch up-close-like. And you should know that she hates dragons."

"I'll not let her hurt him. I promise. I'll do everything I can to protect him. She . . ." William raised his head as what he was about to say struck him. "She needs my help."

He laid his hand on his chest. He suddenly felt lighter. *She needs me! That's right!* He was not without some sort of hold over her. Morga wanted that heirloom for her daughter. She wanted it soon! She'd pushed him to get started on the spell by hurting Pinch. If she waited for Pinch to get old enough to do the tasks, it would take years.

The witch hadn't retaliated when he'd shoved her away from Pinch, nor when he'd snapped at her in the heart of the Old Forest. And the grimwyrms had not attacked him, just Pinch. Yes . . . yes! She needed him.

Morga would get her flames. And after one more task, the witch would go. Already he was thinking ahead to the third task. Maybe, just maybe, he *would* be able to sweep this evil back out the door. Maybe he could undo his stupidity at inviting it in.

He went to his mother's side. She had not cried since she'd given him her love's light, but there was a warmth about her that seemed to make her skin glow.

"I wasn't sure I could do this, Ma. But now I think I can. Soon, Ma."

But tying a tiny strip of cloth over the eyes of a creature barely bigger than a grasshopper was almost impossible! The cloth kept covering his fire-breathing snout. Why was it that sometimes the easiest-sounding thing to do was actually the hardest?

After about twenty tries, William managed to wrap a piece of string several times around Squarmy's eyes. "Well . . ." William scratched his head. "Don't jump around, and maybe it won't come undone."

Carefully, Tuli placed Squarmy on William's palm.

"This'll work," William said. The dragon didn't burn him, but his little feet felt hot. "Should we practice the flames?"

Squarmy snorted a tiny red flame from his nose. Then he opened his mouth and another came out.

William jerked. It was hotter when the flames appeared. But he could bear it for a time. "Fine!" he said. "Let's get this over with quickly. You'd better go," he told Tuli.

William quieted his flip-flopping stomach. He could feel Squarmy shaking. "Shh! It'll be fine. But if you feel you need to, run away as fast as you can."

He cleared his throat and raised his hand. "*Redder than blood are flames that will brand.* Come! I have thirteen for Morga—clutched in bare hand."

Her eyes glared as she stepped into the room. "Ugh! Get that dragon out of my sight! Better yet, throw it on the floor and let me step on it. Filthy pestilence." She raised a hand.

As her hand swung out to swat the dragon, William stepped to the side. He cupped his other hand lightly over Squarmy. He could feel the small creature's panic.

"N-n-n-o-o-o! Don't touch him."

"What?" The witch's spit sprayed him as she spoke. Her face turned red. It matched her eyes, her hair and her gown. She raised both her hands on long arms and extended her clawed fingers.

William was trembling so hard he thought he'd collapse. He didn't. "You—you want your toy, don't you?"

Morga paused. She wiped the spittle from her mouth. "It was that . . . that hideous thing! I detest dragons. I can hardly stand to breathe their stench. When we get rid of the last one, the world will be a better place. I don't know how you can even touch it." She leaned in to peer at him, and he could smell her sulfurous breath. "How *can* you hold it in your bare hand? They would burn the skin of any other human."

"I'm not sure," William admitted. "But I have thirteen flames."

"You're supposed to have the flames in your bare hand for the finding spell to work."

"I do have the flames in my bare hand," William said,

just as a small red flare shot out between his fingers. "Squarmy makes them, but the flames are in my bare hand for a moment."

While Morga seemed to think about this, William twitched. The flame inside his cupped hands had been hotter than he expected. He clenched his jaw. Would he be able to stand thirteen of them?

Finally, Morga announced, "I must say, you've a certain inventive imagination. The heart of the Old Forest, and now this."

William gulped. "It—it will work."

"One thing I know for sure," the witch said as she sidled up close to William. "I have to swallow the flames." She bared her pointed teeth. "I've never tasted dragon, but our elders said they were delicious."

chapter 31

"**R**aise your hand a bit, and I'll open my mouth." The witch licked her lips with her black tongue.

"No!" William cried. "The spell says *thirteen flames*. It doesn't say one dragon. If you swallow Squarmy, you won't get your thirteen flames. You need those."

"Humph!" Morga snorted and stalked away.

William could feel Squarmy running in circles. "Shh... shh," he said as the dragon's tiny heart pounded fiercely against William's skin.

"Do you want your thirteen flames?" he asked Morga as she paced nearby.

"Anxious to get it over with, are you?" she said. "Well, I am, too. I can't abide the smell of this place. Dragons! And Tuli and his spit bucket. Ugh! Very well. I'll have to place my mouth near the side of your hand and swallow the flames as they come out, and before they disappear." She raised a finger. "Don't touch me! I can't stand human filth."

"Fine. But you can't hurt Squarmy!"

Morga threw back her head and laughed. Then she crossed her heart and raised a hand. "I won't hurt that disgusting dragon. And look, I didn't even cross my fingers! Satisfied?"

There wasn't anything more William could do. He'd have to be on guard. She'd fallen to the ground after she'd drunk love's light. Perhaps she'd do that again. And Moggety had said that the fae always honored their promises.

He nodded and lifted his hands. "I'll do the counting," he told Squarmy. "Are you ready? I'll keep you safe." William shot a glance at Morga.

The witch smiled. Then she bent toward him and pursed her lips near his cupped hands.

"Now!" William said. A tiny flame shot out, lighting and heating the skin between his fingers.

Morga sucked it up. She winced.

"One," William counted.

With each flame William's hands grew hotter, and he grew dizzier. His fingers were knit together so tightly above Squarmy, his knuckles were white. By the count of nine, he was kneeling on the floor. And Morga, by his

side, clutched her stomach and shook violently. But she waited for more.

At the count of thirteen, the witch snarled and reared up. She grabbed William by the hair and lifted him straight up from the floor, shaking him—hard. Was she trying to make him drop Squarmy? But she'd promised . . .

Then her red eyes rolled until all William could see were the whites of them. She collapsed in a heap and began to writhe.

William fell to the floor. He scooted away, kicking his feet out. When his back hit a wall, he opened his hands and a yellow blur darted away.

William clutched his throbbing head. But he could

not stop watching Morga. He was mesmerized by her red gown. As the white one had, it quivered with light. Only, this one looked as if blood was coursing through its fabric. Finally, the witch came to rest. She lay on the floor panting.

William did not offer to help her.

Slowly, Morga got to her feet. She shook herself and swept her hands along her skirts.

"You tried to harm Squarmy, and you promised not to!"

The witch sneered. "I did not make a sacred vow. I simply used one of your childish human promises. Crossing your heart . . . as if that means anything." She shrugged. "You poor thing, did your parents never teach you about lying? It's a useful tool."

"Aggh!" Suddenly, Morga stumbled. She threw out an arm and caught herself against one of the archways. She grimaced. "You wonder why I endure such pain? It's all for my daughter, my radiant thirteenth! With my help, she'll be the greatest of the fae folk. She'll rise to take the place that's been denied me."

Still shaking, she walked toward his mother. "Such a pity. Apparently, she didn't love you enough to suffer for you, the way I do for my children. Selfish to leave you to fend for yourselves, wouldn't you say?"

William had no energy to reply. He cradled his head. Still, he kept his eyes on the witch.

Morga's lip curled in disgust. "And speaking of lying, did Tuli ever tell you that he's not truly a guardian? The fae elders got something right, for a change. They didn't appoint him, as they did the others. That's right; my esteemed elders are the ones who arrange for guardians. Pah!" She waved a hand in the air. "An ill-advised pact they made with humans ages ago so we fae could concern ourselves more with the unseen world—our world—than the seen world. But just wait until my daughter takes her place. Then the fae will control both worlds. And there'll be an end to guardians. Dragons, too. And as to that muddleheaded Tuli . . ." She turned, sweeping her hand through the air. "He found this place and just decided to stay, since your poor mother—*his lady*—had no one else. Guardian, hah!" She snickered.

"Well, your last task is the most difficult. Don't fail me, or I'll find Pinch. That herb-woman won't be able to protect him."

Morga turned and raised her arms. "One is done, and two is, too. But three . . . we'll see, shan't we?" Then she ducked under the ivy. "By the way," she said over her shoulder, "you'll regret letting that filthy dragon live!"

Book III

For generations the royal children were protected from the cursed trinket by kindhearted guardians, fairies and dragons.

Oh, yes.

Until one day when a finger was pricked, and a princess slept.

But ofttimes, it is the smallest among us who have the strength to challenge the greatest evil.

And so it was. . . .

chapter 32

William staggered outside. Nearby, one of Squarmy's rainstorms had created another puddle. William fell down and splashed the rainwater over his head. He was still alive.

He stared up at the stars. The cold cleanness of the night air washed over him as he tried to calm himself. When he returned to the building, a light flickered.

"Well done!" Tuli exclaimed. "You did it. And I'm right proud of Squarmy, I am!"

William nodded. "Yes. Thank you, Squarmy. I know how frightened you were."

Squarmy flared and then slipped around Tuli's hand, circling.

When the dragon settled, Tuli reported, "He says he did his duty. And he's going to take a nap, right after he lights a fire for us. He's tuckered out."

William yawned. "I'm exhausted, too."

While Tuli and Squarmy lit the fire, William inspected his hands. They ached a bit, but they'd withstood the ordeal. William closed his eyes and tilted his head back against the wall.

He heard Tuli whistle for Squarmy and then he heard him clear his throat. "Gahhh!"

William opened his eyes.

Tuli was patting his beard. Then the little fellow raised his chin and took a deep breath. "I have something to say. Well, it's just . . . it's just to say *thank you* for taking care of Squarmy." Tuli dabbed at his eyes. "Don't tell the rascally knave, but I don't know what I'd do without him!" He sniffed. "I don't know if I could have held on to him the way you did, what with that witch a-dangling you in the air by your hair." Tuli paused and threw his shoulders back. "And . . ."

"And?" William could barely keep his eyes open.

"Andwhatshesaidistrueaboutmenotreallybeinga guardian." Tuli stopped to take a breath. "I'm sorry! I did not exactly tell the truth. And I didn't like what I heard her say about lying. So there it is."

"There what is?" William yawned again. "What was that you said?"

"Grr!" Tuli growled. "Are you going to make me repeat it?"

"I didn't understand you. Can you say it slower?"

Tuli crumpled in upon himself. He muttered, "What . . . she . . . said . . . is . . . true . . . about . . . me . . . not . . . really . . . being . . . a . . . guardian." He added, "Of course, it be only a wee thing what's stopped me."

William stared at Tuli. Somehow, he'd known that Morga had spoken truthfully.

"It's all right," William said. "You're still—"

"Zounds!" Tuli shouted. He threw his arms up. "Don't press me so hard! It's that I can't count, what's kept me from being a guardian. There! I said it." Tuli hung his head and tugged at the few wisps of hair on top of it. "I know the names of my numbers; I just can't get them in the right order. Squarmy and me been working on it. I know three"—Tuli held up four fingers—"comes after two."

William was silent for a moment. "I was only going to say that I don't care if you didn't get picked by the fae to be a guardian. You're my friend."

Tuli's blue eyes glinted. "You don't mind that I'm not a real guardian?"

"Haven't you watched over my mother? And the fae put up the hedge to guard her, and keep you company. I'd say they found you worthy."

Tuli's brow furrowed. "Aye . . . you're right about the fae. They did do that."

"And haven't you watched out for me?"

"Aye!"

"So I think you're a *real* guardian."

"I guess I am!" Tuli banged his cudgel on the floor.

William sneezed and closed his eyes.

"William, one more thi—"

"Shh!" William waved a finger. "I need to sleep."

"Oh! All right. I'll just sit here and guard." Tuli quieted down, except for an occasional "I'm still here, guarding. I'm here . . . I'm still right here . . . I'm . . . here . . ."

But Tuli was *not* there the next morning.

By Tuli's spittoon and cudgel lay his clothes in a pile. At the sight of them, William felt his heart squeeze up. "Tuli?" He gently lifted the rags and shook them. No Tuli. "Squarmy?" He ducked through an archway, calling, "Lorna-Belle!"

William looked up, and his mouth dropped open.

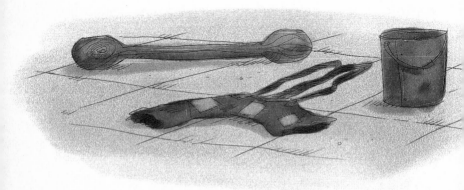

chapter 33

The hedge was so tall William could not see the top of it. *What in the world!*

When he'd gathered his wits again, he quit gaping at the hedge and took a turn around the clearing. He glanced into the swales that pocked the ground. There was no sign of Tuli, or the others. Had Morga come back and taken them? She'd warned him that he'd regret keeping Squarmy alive.

He glanced over his shoulder at the building, wishing more than ever that his mother would wake and help him. He did not want to be alone. He walked back to her side and kissed her cheek.

"I don't know where Tuli and the others are," he told her. "I don't know what to do. I don't know if Morga has done something to them."

He put one of his hands over hers, which were folded as though in prayer. Her skin seemed to glow. If she would just wake up and help him . . .

The longer he thought about his missing friends, the angrier he got. All of this was because of a silly toy—the loss of his father, his mother sleeping. And what about his friends? He slapped the side of the glass bed. Morga needed him if she wanted that heirloom. He whirled around and screamed, "Morga! Morga!"

She came with a brown shawl about her. She did not look pleased.

"Where are they?" he demanded.

"Who?"

"Tuli and Squarmy. And Lorna-Belle."

"How should I know?"

"Because you did something with them, that's why!" He balled up his fists. He was determined that she'd answer his question if she wanted his help. "Tell me, or . . . or I'll not work on the third task!"

"You will! Or you'll never see your precious Pinch again."

"Pinch won't be able to help you for years." William shook the hair out of his eyes. He wouldn't let her scare him. "Don't you want this spell worked before the celebration of your thirteenth daughter's name day?"

Morga strode up and down the small space. "You know nothing about the sacred name days of the fae folk. We celebrate them when it's time to pass on the power. There is no one particular day, as you silly humans seem to have."

William's breath came swooshing out of him. He'd been sure she was in a hurry. "I—I can still take my time with the last task. And I will, unless you tell me where my friends are."

"Silence!" Morga shrieked. "You called me here for this—this foolishness? Who do you think I am, to be called by you whenever you've a need? I have no idea where your useless friends are. Good riddance, I say. Maybe you'll spend more time working on the last task without their interference."

She sneered at him. "And you *will* hurry," she said. "After all, I have only daughters. I might want to raise a son for a change. And I know where to get one—one who still doesn't have a proper name. I could snatch him and name him myself. I quite like that idea. Maybe I'll name him after my father. I could do that, you know? Even *while* you are working on the last task. So don't tempt me!"

William staggered.

"Then, one day, he will oblige his *new mother* without fuss. Hmm . . ." At the archway, she said, "Waste no more time worrying about Tuli and the others. Fair-weather friends, I'd call them, blown this way and that whenever a small problem presents itself. The third task is still to be done. Soon! Or I'll get Pinch and raise him as my own."

As she left, she said, *"Blacker than night is death's icy kindle. Thirteen for Morga—fixed on a spindle."*

Whinnee . . . Aw-ah-aw!

"Lorna-Belle!" William ran around the hedge as she came down the ridge from the Old Forest. He started to hug her.

She whinnied and backed away.

"Is something wrong? Where's Tuli and Squarmy?"

She nudged William and nickered.

"What is it? Are you hurt?" He inspected the mule. "Your sore spot is all scabbed over. That looks all right." Then he saw that her mane had soot-blackened patches in it. "What's happened?"

Lorna-Belle gave a shake. Something yellow tumbled out of her mane.

William knelt and saw Squarmy running in circles. "Squarmy!" He scooped the dragon into his hands. He was hot to the touch, but William could hold him.

William looked from the dragon to Lorna-Belle's mane. Parts of it had definitely been burned. "What's going on? Where's Tuli?"

Squarmy sat up, stretching himself as tall as he could.

William put his face down close to Squarmy and

squinted. There was a bump on the dragon's head. "Did you get hurt?"

The bump jumped.

"Oh! Is that a flea on you? Hold still and I'll pick it off."

Squarmy began to frantically circle and bob all over William's hand.

"Hold still! How can I get it off you if you don't hold still?"

And then William heard a tiny squeak. What was that? It seemed to be coming from Squarmy. Was Squarmy trying to talk to him? William had never been able to understand the dragon, but if Squarmy was trying to say something, he'd do his best to listen. "All's well. Calm down. Tell me what the problem is." William put his hand up close to his ear to hear Squarmy.

Something tickled his ear! The bug that had been on Squarmy must have leapt off the dragon and onto him. He raised his other hand to slap it.

"Ouch!" Squarmy bit him! Then the dragon leapt and grabbed a lock of William's hair.

William sucked at the nip to his hand as his head tickled. "Why'd you do that?"

Now, he didn't want to go scratching about on his head in case he accidentally swatted Squarmy. But he was getting itchy, and his scalp still hurt from Morga's tugging on it. Then he smelled hair burning. Was Squarmy setting his head on fire?

He heard the tiny squeak again. This time, it came from near his ear. He closed his eyes to concentrate. Could it be? It sounded like . . . "Tuli?" William whispered. "Tuli, is that you?"

The tickling near his ear increased. Squarmy jumped from William's head onto one of his hands. He bobbed up and down.

"That's impossible," William whispered. Tuli was as small as a flea?

Then he felt something cross his cheek and jump onto his nose. He closed one eye and looked sideways. He could just spy the tip of his nose, and a dab of red. Tuli's beard!

It *was* Tuli!

Out of the corner of his eye, William saw the towering hedge. He heaved a deep sigh and felt a small pinch on the end of his nose.

chapter 34

William's sigh had almost shaken Tuli off into the wind! That must have been what had happened. Tuli had shrunk, and the wind had carried him away. And then . . . *yes.* The others had gone to find him.

William cupped one hand like a barrier wall before his nose—not touching Tuli. With the other hand, he patted his head to be sure his hair wasn't completely on fire.

Now they had to find a safe place for Tuli, at least until tomorrow, when he might be bigger. William searched the small building, and Squarmy helped. It had to be a place where Tuli could not be blown about.

William stopped. Blown about by the wind? What was it Morga had said? *Fair-weather friends, I'd call them, blown this way and that* . . . and something about a *small problem.* She *had* known what had happened to his friends! William ground his teeth as they searched.

They considered Tuli's spit bucket. But what if the wind tipped it over, or rain got in it and drowned Tuli? No. They looked under the glass bed. They had to hide Tuli somewhere *absolutely* safe.

William looked at his mother's folded hands. They reminded him of his own hands protecting Squarmy from the witch. Perhaps? Gently, he pried open the space where her two hands met. There was a little gap.

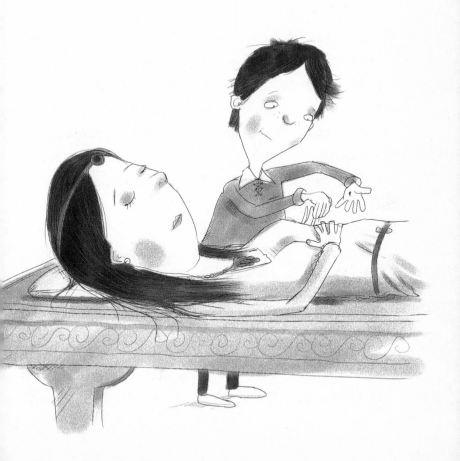

"You'll be safe in my mother's hands," William said.

William felt a tingling on his nose. He wasn't sure if Tuli was agreeing or not. But he lowered the one hand he'd used as a protective barrier and leaned in toward his mother. A speck scurried into the dark space between his mother's hands.

"Whew!" William really needed to rub his tickly nose. He kept an eye on Squarmy as he raised a finger. The dragon did not seem to be concerned. Good! William scratched. *Ahh!*

With Tuli safe, he worked on his third task. *Blacker than night is death's icy kindle. Thirteen for Morga—fixed on a spindle.* For the other tasks, the witch hadn't needed the thimble, or Squarmy. She'd needed thirteen drops of love's light, and the thirteen flames. So it seemed like the important part was the thirteen bits of kindling.

A spindle hung downward and spun so that wool could be wound around it. It had a shaft. And around that shaft, near one end, was a platform, or whorl, that the shaft was stuck through. How was he going to get icy kindling fixed to one of those? And what was icy kindling? You couldn't kindle a fire with ice.

Spindles always reminded him of tops. He had played with one at home when he was younger, spinning it around and around, until his mother had abruptly taken it away from him. It made a fun toy . . . *toy!* William jumped up. It was a toy that Morga had lost. Perhaps

Tuli was right and the spindle in the last task was the toy Morga wanted? Moggety had mentioned the spindle as well. So was this task different, then? Maybe it wasn't the thirteen bits of kindling that were important; maybe it was the spindle itself?

William paced, trying to remember everything the witch had said. She'd claimed his mother had stolen it. Why would William's mother do that? She had a spindle at home, and she was not a thief. And if, as Tuli claimed, Morga was the uninvited fairy at Princess Bree's name-day celebration, then the spindle had to be the one from the story—the one that was meant to kill the princess.

If that was so, then, somehow, he had to find it and . . . and do what? Stick icy kindling all over it? But Moggety had said not to touch it. William put his head in his hands. How would he *ever* be able to do this task? In the first place, he didn't have the spindle. And what was *icy* kindling? Icicles?

Maybe he would have to go back up Crag Angorm. That was the only place there would be ice this time of year. Then he remembered that the ice needed to kindle death. Could an icicle cause death? He supposed if you stabbed someone with an icicle, it might. He shivered.

Perhaps he was forgetting something? For the first task, he'd forgotten the trembling. He repeated the spell out loud.

Whiter than snow is love's light atremble.
Thirteen for Morga—scooped in a thimble.

Redder than blood are flames that will brand.
Thirteen for Morga—clutched in bare hand.

Blacker than night is death's icy kindle.
Thirteen for Morga—fixed on a spindle.

That was it; three tasks. But something was nagging at him. There had been more to the spell than just the tasks. Oh, yes. He'd almost forgotten the last part. How did that go?

A thimble of love.
A handful of flame.
A spindle of death.
And I'll go whence I came.

He'd given her a thimble of love. He'd given her a handful of flame. So he just had to give her—he gulped and leapt up. Now he knew what had to be on that spindle—and he needed thirteen of them . . . thirteen deaths.

He ran his hand through his hair. How was he going to do that? Of one thing he was certain: it couldn't be just any spindle. He had to find the one that had been meant for Princess Bree.

chapter 35

William kissed his mother good night.
"I'll figure it out, somehow," he said. Then he touched
her hands and added, "Good night, Tuli."

The first thing William saw the next morning was
Tuli. He was about Pinch's size again. And he was curled
around his spittoon with his clothes on.

"Tuli, wake up!"

Tuli yawned and stretched. "Well, that was an ad-
venture! Thanks be Lorna-Belle was here. Otherwise, it
takes me days to get back. Blasted wind blew me almost
to the river."

"You've been that small before?"

"Aye. More'n once I've had to hide till the next day."
Tuli raised a hand to pat his beard and stopped. "What?"
He opened his hand. Inside was a small key. "Aye, that's

right! I remember." He held the key out. "I found this in my lady's hand. Right cold it was to curl up against."

William took the key. It was small and made of silver. He wondered aloud, "What does it open?"

Tuli said, "I think it opens a lock."

"Of course it does!" William retorted before he had time to catch himself.

"Don't be getting short with me! You're not the one that had to keep his self from getting splatted against a tree. Believe me, it fuddle-tweaks your thinking for a day or two."

"I'm sorry. Of course, it must." He hadn't meant to be rude. "Are you all right? I was worried."

"Aye! Just be getting my wits back. They'll get all sorted soon."

"Good." William twirled the key. "Now, there's got to be a keyhole somewhere."

Together they searched inside and out. They even inspected his mother's cushion, her gown, the circlet of jewels and the locket she wore. Not a keyhole anywhere.

William opened the locket. Inside was a portrait of Da. He thought back to the last time he'd seen his father. He'd seemed distant, as if something was on his mind. And Moggety had said that on his last visit he wasn't talkative. She thought he was hiding something from her. Hiding something—some . . . *thing*?

William began to pace.

Tuli interrupted him. "You're making me dizzy."

"I'm thinking that I might have to leave for a while."

"You are?" Tuli's lip began to quiver.

"I think my da had something on him that the key might fit into. I'm sorry, Tuli."

Tuli grabbed his spit bucket.

"Please don't put your bucket on your head. I want to talk to you. I'll need your help. That is, your lady still needs you to guard her."

"Well, I ain't saying as how I'll miss you. But . . ." Tuli put the spittoon on his head.

William sighed. "Tuli, come out. Please!"

Slowly, Tuli took the bucket off. His head was dripping.

William tried not to look at it. "I have to go back to the village. I think my father may have had something on him, something that this key is for. I'll see if any of Da's friends found anything on him before they buried—" William stopped. No! Morga had found the lock of hair Da always kept in his pocket. So she had gotten to him first.

He straightened up and rubbed his chin. If Morga had gone through his father's pockets, she'd have kept whatever she found. And if she'd found something that needed a key, she'd have looked here, around his mother, for the key—just as she'd looked for the spindle. No. He was certain that whatever it was, Morga did not have it. So it must not have been on his father when he fell. That meant he must have done something with it before he fell from . . .

Cliven Rock! That was why Da went there. Now it made sense!

Da had had something with him on his last trip, and he hadn't told Moggety. Then he went up to Cliven Rock to hide it. He hadn't been there to work on the first task. It had never seemed right to William that his father had gotten the first task all wrong.

And he knew just where his father had hidden what he'd carried! Cliven Rock was a round boulder that looked as if it had been almost cut in two, with its halves splayed open like a split egg—balanced on the very edge of the cliff. Down between the two halves, where it was still connected, was a scooped-out spot. *Yes!* Da had hidden something in Cliven Rock.

Quickly, William readied his bedroll. He would go to Cliven Rock and find what Da had hidden. Before he left, he kissed his mother good-bye. Tuli had given his word that he'd continue to guard her.

Tuli had his bucket on his head again. But a blue eye peeked out, and fat tears zigzagged down his cheeks.

William knelt. "Tuli, you are my friend. Living on top of the mountain, I never had a chance to make friends. I will miss you. But I *will* come back. I promise." William touched the small fellow's shoulder.

Tuli leaned forward, and the bucket dropped all the way down on his head. Still, he managed to reach out and hug William.

chapter 36

William stopped by the graveyard. "Da, I brought this for you." He pulled out the lock of Ma's hair. He wrapped it in a strip of cloth from his shirt and buried it near his father's grave. "You always carried it. You should have it now. I've found her, and we'll be reunited soon . . . Pinch, and Ma, and me. So you don't need to worry." Then he wiped his eyes and rode across the bridge, through the high meadows and into the chill mountain air.

It didn't surprise William that Pinch and Moggety were waiting to greet him. Somehow, Moggety knew when anyone was coming along the path.

"Pinch!" William slid off Lorna-Belle and grabbed his brother. Then Moggety hugged William. Lirian and Heldor rubbed against his legs. And William introduced Lorna-Belle.

HELDOR
A
FRIEND
R·I·P

"May I ride her?" Pinch asked. "Please! Please!"

"Well, she's tired. And—" William was stopped by a nudge. "Um, I guess it's fine with her."

He lifted Pinch to the mule's back. "Hey! You look almost normal." William laughed. "The bite marks have disappeared. Now, hold on."

Early the next morning, William told Moggety about his mother, about Morga and about the tasks. And he told her about Tuli and Squarmy. She raised an eyebrow at that.

Then he thanked her for coming to his rescue in the

Old Forest. "It worked! You were there with me when I held the vial. I mean, your sending was. I could see you as clearly as I saw Morga pretending to be you by your fire."

"But crumpelstilts, if you didn't give me a right hard place to get to! No less a place than the heart of the Old Forest! I wasn't sure I could hold back all that deep energy. 'Tis a green force that always wins in the end. But you got away. Thank goodness the wee one was napping at the time. It took all my strength to get that sending to work. Here, at the cottage, a fly could have knocked me over."

"Oh!" William furrowed his brow. "I'm sorry. I didn't know it would take . . . I mean, I didn't know it would affect you like that."

"Ach! I'm rusty on sendings, that's all. Haven't used one in years. There now." She patted him on the knee. "Not to worry. Go on with your telling."

Then he told her he had to go to Cliven Rock.

Moggety shook her head. "'Tis not safe—the snow is deep up the crag. And your father fell there. How are you going to keep from going over, too?"

She chewed at her lower lip. "Howsoever, I'd wager that you're right about Heldor hiding something there. For it seems to me now that he was protective of his pack on that last visit. I'd supposed, at the time, that he had some little thing in it for you and the wee one. Now

I see that it might be otherwise. If it be that fae spindle, I've no idea how your da got ahold of it."

William piped up, "I'll be extra careful on the ledge."

"I'm sure Heldor was careful, too. Still, I can't see any way around it but to retrieve what he's hidden. For I'm afraid I can't protect the wee one from that witch every moment of the day. She's sure to pull some trickery and get Pinch away from my side if that finding riddle isn't worked through. Blathers!" Moggety spit out that last word, red-faced and angry. "Her and that spindle! I'm sure that's what put Lirian to sleep. It sounds like it from everything you've told me."

"Do you think it's the same one from the old story? Tuli says Morga was the witch at Princess Bree's celebration."

"Aye," Moggety said. "I'm afraid so. That witch unearthed an old fae spindle with death on it and tried to give it to baby Bree."

William thought of his mother in the dainty building. Had she known it would put her in a deep sleep? Still, he didn't know if he truly believed that his mother was of the royal family. It seemed . . . well, it just seemed too strange to be true.

"What you might not know," Moggety continued before William could ask anything else, "is that Morga swore vengeance upon her sisters." She shifted a bit and leaned in. "I'm not certain, mind you, but it's said she placed curses for her sisters on that thing, to boot.

"So the good fairies hid it. Over the years I've had many an uneasy feeling about it. I'd say that, somehow or other, the spindle made its way to the Old Forest, for that's where Lirian is." Moggety put her head in her hands. "Ach! So much pain caused by such a wee blithering trinket." Her shoulders slumped.

William reached out and put a hand on her arm.

A bit later, he cleared his throat and said, "Tuli told me something, but it's so . . ." He stopped. It sounded so silly—it just didn't fit. He took his hand from Moggety's shoulder. "Tuli said my mother was a princess, a descendant of Princess Bree's. So that would mean I'm some sort of prince. But I think Tuli got that wrong. He can get mixed up. *Addle-tweaked,* he calls it."

"Ha! That Tuli sounds right interesting." Moggety's response was exactly as William had thought it might be. She leaned back, laughing.

William shrugged, a bit relieved.

Then Moggety added, "Howsoever, he's right. You *are* a prince. Pinch, too. Your mother is a princess. And your grandfather is our king."

William slid off the bench and landed on the floor.

chapter 37

Moggety winked. "Oh, aye, Your Royal Highness! Sitting on my floor like a startled wee coney. What tales you'll have to tell your children one day!" She slapped the tabletop.

William's brain was whirling. He did feel like a startled rabbit. He had a grandfather who was the king? And he *really* was a—a prince? But how could that be? He'd been so sure Tuli was wrong. He stared into Moggety's eyes, speechless, as she helped him up to the bench.

"The sad bit is," Moggety continued as though nothing much had happened, "that Lirian, our dear princess, found that evil spindle. Morga has searched far and wide for the royal children, but the dragons, and the guardians, were good at keeping them safe." Moggety lifted a ladle of water to William's mouth and waited as he sipped it.

She shook her head. "It was up on the crag that your mother longed to live out her days with those she loved. The king, your grandfather, was going to name a steward as heir, someone not related. Your mother was willing to give up the throne. They'd hoped that would put a stop to it. It's been a great sorrow that each generation of royal children had to be hidden until there was a next generation."

Moggety tightened her jaw. "But it sounds like that evil thirteenth daughter came snooping around the mountain once your dragon was gone. And the only way your mother knew to save you, and Pinch, was to put an end to the curse that awaited the king's heirs by finding and destroying the spindle. Or . . ."

"Or?"

Moggety bit her lip. "Ach! I'm just an old woman rambling a bit. One thing's for certain, Lirian must have touched it." Moggety rummaged around among some nearby baskets. "She may have used up the royal curse by touching the spindle. But sure as I'm standing here, I've a bad feeling there are other curses on that thing."

Over her shoulder she added, "And now your mother, my lady, sleeps in the deepest part of the Old Forest, while our good king mourns."

Moggety turned and looked him in the eye. "And the king worries about you and Pinch, too."

"He—he does?"

"Crumpelstilts! Of course he does. You two are his grandsons. Didn't my cottage look a wee bit familiar?" She waited for William's answer, her hands on her hips.

It had . . . there *was* something. William closed his eyes and sniffed. Maybe it was the way it smelled? He had a long-ago memory of some kind of coziness that felt safe and warm, and he'd been somewhere on the mountain that wasn't their home. "Have I been here before?"

"Aye. When you were a babe. Lirian and Heldor would come down to meet your grandparents here. It was a safe place for the royal couple to travel to in disguise, and always just the king and queen dressed as beggars. No others, in case it drew attention.

"When you got older, your mother would only bring Pinch. She didn't want you finding out about your royal blood—not yet. Then, not long after Pinch was born, the queen died. It was right hard on your mother not to attend the royal funeral, I can tell you. Too dangerous! It's certain that Morga would have been there searching for royal family members among the crowd. After the queen died, the king got tired in his soul, I think. He hasn't visited since afore your mother went away." Moggety wiped her hands on her apron. "And now it's fallen to me to tell you what should have been your mother's tale to tell."

"I remember that sometimes she'd only take Pinch on her back. She never returned with many supplies. Just a few herbs, or vials . . ." William glanced around the walls of the cottage.

"I—I thought she was just going down for supplies again, that last time. She turned and waved to us. I didn't know that I'd not see her for . . ." He trailed off and was silent while Moggety bustled about. Finally, he asked, "Should we let the king know what's happened? I mean, about the tasks and all?"

"Nay. He's got his ways of knowing. There be watchful guardians all over the kingdom; the good fae saw to that." Moggety picked up a wooden spoon. She pointed it at William. "The way I've got it figured is, it was our king that built that pretty little chapel for Lirian. And the good fae folk are keeping a thorn hedge there to protect the royal heir. But it sounds like it might be a bit addled itself—sprouting up and down as Tuli does. Or the other way around. Ofttimes, when the human world and fae world cross paths, things can get a wee bit, well, *addle-tweaked*—as you said Tuli gets sometimes."

Moggety took a pot off the fire. "The king cannot come to help you. It would only anger Morga more. She is much more powerful than a simple man who happens to be a king. I think he's done what he could, at his age. Now the rest is up to you." She looked William in the eyes. "And me. I'll do my best. I'm putting my mind onto thinking about Cliven Rock, as we speak."

She set plates on the table. "But the first thing I can do is to get you fed. Then I'll get you outfitted to tackle that ledge. And mayhap I've a thing or two that might come in handy."

When he'd finished his breakfast, William thrust his shoulders back. "I have to tell Pinch I'm leaving again."

Moggety chuckled. "Keep your arms and legs clear of his fists. It's hard for him. He's afraid of losing you. In the meantime, I'll get things together. That witch belittles the natural world, but sometimes it's the simple things that can help the most."

chapter 38

Lorna-Belle carried a long sturdy pole, rope and a couple of heavy pouches that Moggety had secured on her. By midafternoon William and the mule were above the tree line. As they climbed higher, there was more and more snow.

Finally, William spied the path to Cliven Rock. He turned Lorna-Belle up the side trail. Farther along, they passed Da's big sledge. It was still laden with snow-covered bundles. William did not stop.

They turned a sharp curve, and abruptly, the world below was spread out spring green and misty-edged. Lorna-Belle shied backward. "All's well." William slid to the ground and pressed himself against the rock wall that ringed the back of the stone balcony. From this protruding lip on the mountainside, the valley was a dizzying sight.

The ledge sloped downward on the left side, toward the two halves of a round boulder with a crack making a gap down its middle—Cliven Rock. The rock was as tall as William, and the two halves spread wider than his outstretched arms. The rock balanced on the very edge of the cliff with an almost magical hold. On the right, the ledge rose upward. And back a bit from the edge on that end was the flat rock where he'd often sat with Ma and Da.

He eased himself over to the rock bench. When they'd picnicked here, he'd been happy, staring out over the wide world. But now all he could think about was his father's battered body lying below.

Soon the wetness of the rock seeped through to his skin. He should do what he'd come to do. He surveyed the stone balcony. It was dusted with a layer of snow, and he could see the sparkle of ice. Also, the crevice in Cliven Rock was packed with snow down where the two halves met. He'd have to rake it out to find anything hidden in there.

Was there something he could secure his rope to? He'd worked out a plan with Moggety, and the first thing they had agreed upon was that he'd tie the rope around his middle.

There were no trees or stumps this high up. And the stone wall, rising behind him, was weathered smooth. He slipped backward off his seat. Could he tie the rope around this flat rock? It was large, but he might be able to stretch his rope all the way around it and still have enough length to walk to the farther end and Cliven Rock.

He pulled the rope off Lorna-Belle and worked it around the base of the rock. His only concern was that the rope might rise and slip off.

Huh? There was a tug on the rope. William twisted around. Lorna-Belle had the rope in her mouth. Maybe that would work! If he could tie the rope around Lorna-Belle, he'd feel safer about stepping out on the downward-sloping end of the ledge.

He looped the rope over her head and around her neck. Then he stuffed under it a blanket Moggety had packed for him, so the rope wouldn't cut into the mule. He tied the other end around his waist and rested his face alongside hers for a moment. "This is it, girl."

Lorna-Belle showed him her teeth. She shook her head.

It was time. He did as they'd planned and hauled up Moggety's chain to clutch the vial. A pale green mist appeared above, on the top of the rock wall that loomed over the ledge. And then . . . Moggety—or rather, a sending of her.

She said, "Split open the pouches."

Still gripping the vial, William did; each pouch held several handfuls of sand. *Simple things,* she'd said, could be the most helpful. He smiled and scattered the sand across the ledge in front of him.

"Take the pole," the sending said.

William splayed himself against the back wall and began to step slowly toward the downward end and Cliven Rock. He'd let go of the vial so he could keep one hand against the wall and use the other hand to wedge the long pole against the rock floor and steady himself. The sand helped his boots get a grip on the slippery surface. Only once did he stumble, when his toe hit a triangular tip of rock, sticking up from the ledge.

He made it to the sloping end. Now it was a matter of stepping outward toward Cliven Rock. Over his shoulder the distant valley lay with its misty arms open. It seemed to be waiting—waiting for him. Had his father felt the same? His stomach screwed up with fear. He tucked the pole between him and the wall and then grabbed the vial.

Moggety called out, "Turn your eyes! Distance always beguiles."

He gulped and forced his eyes from the valley. Cliven Rock sat four or five good paces from the back wall— right out on the edge of the protruding lip. He let go of the vial again so he could hang on to the wall with one hand and stretch out his pole with the other; it barely reached the cleft in the rock. He jabbed it forward to see if there was some way to clear the snow and tug out whatever was hidden there. The snow was packed hard. He thrust once more, and the pole flew from his hand, disappearing over the edge in a heartbeat. *Oh, no!*

There was no way around it. He'd have to step out, away from the wall. If he slid, he would aim himself at the back of the rock, where he would be safe.

He found the vial. "I lost the pole," he told the sending of Moggety. "I have to walk to the rock."

"No!" the sending cried. "Come back and—"

"I can't come this far and not try my best. It's only a few steps away, and the sand helps. I'm tied on." Then he let go of the vial to stretch his arms out for balance. Moggety was gone.

William's stomach clenched up. He took one step. He looked at Lorna-Belle. She had her eyes on him.

He took another step, and another—picking out the sandiest places to put his feet. He took two more steps. Almost there. One more and he'd be able to touch the back of the rock. If he just leaned a bit . . . maybe he could grab at it now. *Swoop!*

He landed on a shoulder and slid—sideways! He grabbed at the rope, turned on his belly and spread his legs, hoping to catch one of his feet against the back of Cliven Rock. But the ledge sloped sharply away at the side of the precariously balanced boulder. He was sliding over . . .

Suddenly, his rope was yanked taut. It cut off

William's breath as it tightened around his waist. His legs dangled in midair, but the top half of him was still on the ledge. He raised his eyes. Lorna-Belle was holding him, her legs firmly planted and her head reared back. Then William saw the loop about her neck jerk off the blanket he'd wedged under it. He slid a few more inches. The rope was beginning to rise up the mule's neck.

With one hand William clutched the rope. With the other he braced his fingers against the slippery floor of the ledge and tried to pull himself up. And then . . . the rope gave a few more inches with a quick loosening and tightening. It must have jumped a bit more up Lorna-Belle's neck.

Now just his arms and elbows were bracing him on the ledge. There was only one thing to do. He would have to put his full weight on the rope, climb up it and hope to make it to safety before the loop slid over Lorna-Belle's head.

"Aiii!" He dropped a little more as the rope took all his weight. Panic-stricken, he flailed his legs wildly. His arms, dragged across the sharp lip of the cliff, were cut by the rough stone.

He began to slide his hands up the rope. First one hand—*Breathe!*—then the other—*Breathe!* He inched himself higher up the rope. His muscles cramped. His arms shook. Hand after hand, elbow after elbow, he dragged himself back onto the floor of the ledge. When he was lying on top, he swung sideways on his belly to the back of Cliven Rock. There he braced both feet at the base of the rock behind him and relaxed his grip on the rope.

Shaking and sobbing, he needed a few minutes before he could raise his head to see Lorna-Belle. The rope was high about her jaw and ears. When he could speak again, he whispered, "Good girl."

At last, with his feet behind him and set against Cliven Rock, he pushed up to his knees. Then he leaned his back against the boulder. Slowly, he turned to catch hold of one half of the rock. Steadying himself against the rock with one hand, he began to brush the snow out of the crevice with the other.

At last, he felt something that wasn't snow or ice. It was hard, and squarish. He pulled a small box out of the cleft and pushed it into his pocket. Then he angled himself around to face the back wall of the ledge. He'd have to pull himself up the sloping shelf—somehow.

He looked at Lorna-Belle. The rope was sitting up around her ears. Despite her head's shaking and the loosening of the rope, it wasn't falling back down her neck. There was nothing William could do but chance that the rope would not fly off her head.

He lay down on his stomach and braced his feet against the base of Cliven Rock. With his arms outstretched, all he needed was a few pulls up the slippery shelf to reach the back wall. He took a deep breath and

then strained forward to find a fingerhold to pull against. There wasn't one.

Lorna-Belle took a step backward. The rope around William tightened. His knees slid forward across the sand. The mule took another step back. The rope slipped a bit, pressing her ears firmly down and forward. Any second now, the rope might lift off her.

William's heart raced as he swept his hands forward and sideways. He could almost touch the back wall! But there was nothing on the smooth surface of the ledge to grab on to.

Lorna-Belle stepped back once more. The rope slipped past her ears and zipped along her muzzle.

chapter 39

"**N**o!" William was sliding. Frantically, he bent his knees and lunged forward. As his head came down, Moggety's chain flew out and snagged itself on the bit of rock by the back wall that he had stubbed his toe on. He was caught by the chain! It dug into the nape of his neck and pinned him against the floor of the ledge.

He couldn't breathe. He stretched a hand up and followed the chain to the spot it was snagged on. He grabbed at that small handhold and, pulling forward, managed to loosen the chain and drag himself to safety at the wall. There he crouched for a long time, clutching at Moggety's vial.

Moggety's sending stood above him, on the top of the wall at his back. "What's happened?" she cried. "What did you do? What's going on?"

"I'm—I'm all right," he said, panting. "I found a box."

At Moggety's, salve was applied to the spots where William had gotten scraped and cut. And then he was put to bed. The next morning, Moggety fed him thick buttery porridge.

William lifted the chain with the small vial. "It was a good sending," he said. "I hope it didn't wear you out like the last one."

"Ach! This one was easy, compared to getting myself all the way to the Old Forest. The botherating part is, I can't know what's going on unless my sendings are there. I think my hair turned all shades of white worrying about what was happening in between the glimpses I got."

"I'm sorry about worrying you. Everything you gave me helped."

"And Lorna-Belle helped, didn't she?" Pinch put in.

"Yes! I tied my rope to her. I owe her an extra-long hug."

"Can I hug her, too?" Pinch asked.

William laughed. "I'm sure she'd like that."

"But first," Moggety said, "we must get a look at what your brother found."

William placed the box on the tabletop. It was only as long as his hand, and thin. The top was covered in tiny white stones. And it had a keyhole on one of the shorter ends.

Moggety studied it. "When you open it, don't touch what's inside." She lifted Pinch and held him tightly.

William put the key in. He started to lift the lid, but Moggety clamped a hand onto his wrist. She shook her head and reached for her wooden spoon.

He used the spoon to flip the lid open. He gasped . . .

Pinch lurched forward. Moggety gripped him so tightly that he cried, "Ow!"

Inside was a jeweled spindle made of crystal—delicate and as tiny as a toy—a *toy* spindle. Its shaft sparkled, and red jewels bedecked its circular whorl. It flickered and begged to be picked up.

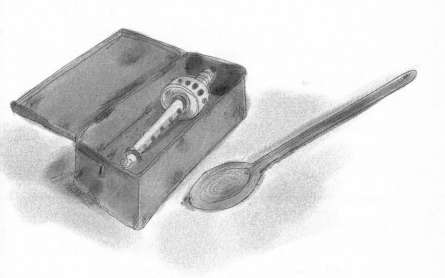

"Don't touch it!" Moggety cried. "Who knows what kind of evil it can do!"

"It's Morga's heirloom," William whispered. "It's so . . . so beautiful!"

"Bah! 'Tis a bad thing." Moggety's voice was trembling. "Do you not see? That black whorl that the red stones sit atop is made of bone—charred bone. And it's human bone or I'm a water nymph! It's what's made your mother fall sleep. And any other curses on it—"

She was interrupted by Pinch. "Mama?" he asked, twisting around to look at Moggety. Then he turned to William, his face going red. "Where's Mama? Is she sleeping?" Pinch tried to get free of Moggety's grip to lunge at his brother. "Where *is* she!"

Moggety rose and struggled to carry a wriggling Pinch from the room. "It's too dangerous to have the wee one near that evil thing. Lock it away!"

She went out the door with Pinch, and William heard her telling his brother that she had a little story for him. It was all about a princess who was very brave and slept in the Old Forest.

William stared at the spindle. After a few moments, he noticed that something seemed to be missing from it. There was a flattened top to the hook at the end of the spindle's shaft. And it looked as if there had once been a large jewel of some sort on that spot, for a dainty edging of silver encircled an empty space.

William counted twelve red jewels. *Hmm . . .* "The missing stone would make thirteen gems." Thirteen!

Blacker than night is death's icy kindle. Thirteen for Morga—fixed on a spindle. Here on the table was the spindle. And Moggety thought there might be more curses on it—curses for each of Morga's twelve sisters. Were there twelve? Or more? He scratched his head.

Ma must have touched it and used one curse. And there was one jewel missing. That made sense. So there were, probably, still twelve curses on it. One for each of the jewels it bore. If there were only twelve, how could he get a thirteenth death on it? He wasn't a fae. He couldn't conjure up a curse on his own. Where would he find another?

William sat for a long time, staring at the spindle. He desperately wanted to touch the beautiful toy—just once. Who would know? Moggety and Pinch were outside. He had the stirring spoon in one hand, but he couldn't bring himself to close the lid.

Suddenly, his seat was jostled. He looked down. The gray kitten had leapt to his side. When he looked back at the box, the lid was closed, and the orange kitten sat on the table calmly licking a paw. Shakily, William looked from Lirian to Heldor on the bench and whispered, "Thank you."

William locked the box. Then he stepped out of the

cottage and listened to the last of Moggety's story. ". . . and her eyelids fluttered open—"

"And were they happy after that?" asked Pinch, interrupting Moggety.

"Oh, aye!" she answered him. "If truth be told, they lived happily ever after."

William clutched his hand around the box. It felt as cold as death.

William and Lorna-Belle left at dawn. This time, William did not stop at the graveyard. Instead, he promised himself that when this was all over, he'd sit by Da's grave and tell his father the whole story. Perhaps Ma would come with him.

In the clearing, the thorn hedge was only as high as Lorna-Belle's belly. Would Tuli be taller? And a good portion of the hedge was green. It was coming back to life.

"Tuli!" William shouted. "Squarmy!"

A man lifted the trailing ivy, ducked his head and came out from the dainty building.

William paused and then laughed. It was a man-sized Tuli!

"You're yelling so loud a body could hear you all the way to the river!" Tuli said. "How's one supposed to think with such a to-do?"

William slid off Lorna-Belle and grabbed Tuli around the middle.

Tuli spluttered.

William didn't care that spit rained down on him.

"A right welcome to you, as well," his friend said. The next moment, a tiny yellow head peeked out of his red beard.

William reached up. A flicker of warmth flowed through him as Squarmy rubbed on the tip of his finger.

As soon as he could, William talked to his mother. "I have the spindle. And I'll do everything I can to make Morga awaken you. I promise." He touched her hair for a moment. "Pinch misses you. I do, too."

chapter 40

William unlocked the box to show Tuli the spindle. Immediately, Squarmy leapt out of Tuli's beard and ran so swiftly around the walls and along the ceiling that he looked like a crazed streak of sunlight.

"Stop that, you rowdy thing!" Tuli began to knock his cudgel about.

"Be careful, Tuli!"

"Ech!" Tuli spit into his bucket. "Just trying to slow him down so's I can ask what's gotten him into such a rude dither." Tuli whistled. *Cher-ick!* Still, it was some time before the dragon sprang into Tuli's beard. "Calm down. Calm down, you hear me!" Tuli turned to William. "I've never seen him this fuddle-whopped." Then he cupped a hand near his ear and consoled Squarmy, "There, there . . ."

William looked at the spindle while Tuli spoke to

Squarmy. Perhaps it was not a good idea to leave the box lying open. He raised his hand and started to touch . . . *No!* He jerked away and shoved his shaking hands into his pockets. He felt Da's knife, and he took a deep breath. Da . . . Then he used the knife to flip the lid closed. He relocked the box.

When William looked up, he saw that Tuli's eyes were wide. His friend was mumbling. "Hmm, hmm, hmm!" And, "Aggh!" Eventually, he turned to William with a grim look. "Best not open your box again. What's inside be dangerous," he said. "Squarmy keeps repeating *evil, evil.*"

William nodded. "Moggety said that, too. What does Squarmy know about the spindle? Are there curses on it? And how many?"

Tuli listened a bit more to Squarmy before answering. "He reckons there be one for each of Morga's good sisters. That be . . ." Tuli paused to try to count on his fingers.

"Twelve," William said.

Tuli continued, "Aye. And she put a curse on it to kill the king's heirs, too. That's part of the old stories. But that one got changed and was spent on my lady."

"So there're twelve deaths still on it." William chewed at the inside of his cheek, thinking. "But Morga wants thirteen deaths. Thirteen exactly."

Tuli interrupted him. "There be something else Squarmy said."

"What?"

"He said something about my da's green stone." Tuli pulled out his wadded-up packet of rags. He unwrapped the stone.

William came closer and stared at the shining beauty. At first, all he could see was its green depths. And then he had a thought. "Tuli! There's a stone missing on the spindle. I was going to show you, but Squarmy got so upset, I closed the box. Your da's stone would fit perfectly!"

William forced himself to turn from the stone and open the box again. "See!" He pointed to the hook below the whorl. "There. It's obvious there was an oval stone that sat in that bracket."

Tuli squinted. "Well, I'll be . . . It does seem like it belongs there. I think there be something Squarmy ain't told me yet."

The room had grown darker, and it began to rain outside.

Tuli put his stone away. Then he cupped his hand over his beard. *Cher-ick!* "Squarmy! Wake up! I know you're exhausted from all your fancy-dancing what-a-doodle, but it's no time to be dreaming of weather. Come here, you mischievating storm-pup!"

The rain stopped. Squarmy poked his head out. Tuli scooped him up in his clenched fist.

"Got you!" Tuli declared as his hand jerked wildly about. "Now, it ain't going to do you any good bashing your skull against my hand. I'm not letting you go until you tell me the whole story, you little thief! William needs to know." Tuli's hand quit its unnatural jerking to and fro. He raised his fist to his ear. "Out with it, you hear?"

Tuli listened to Squarmy for a few moments before William saw big tears coursing down the fellow's cheeks. Then Tuli whispered into his hand, "I'm right sorry I ever doubted you, my friend. And to think I been calling you a cutpurse and worse. On my ma's cudgel, I promise to never call you a thief again. I wished you'd have told me this afore." Tuli sniffed and placed his hand up by his beard. "There you go. You're a tired lad. Go dream about some pretty lightning."

Tuli had a pleased look. "Well, I'm right proud of Squarmy, I am."

"Why?"

"It turns out he *had to* try to steal my da's stone. It was the good fae what ordered the dragons to keep a watch for it. You see, dragons are neither fae nor human. So at Princess Bree's name-day celebration, the queen of the dragons pried that stone off the spindle and carried it away. That turned Morga's killing curse into a sleeping one. It has to be put all together to kill.

"When Squarmy saw me sitting on your mountain with that green stone, he got all wally-kinked with worry. He didn't know if he should stay and guard your family or follow the stone and make sure it never got back onto the spindle. Well, he jumped in my pocket, and he's kept an eye on the thing ever since."

Tuli scratched his head. "He never told me this 'cause he's always been worried if he made the right choice. He's ashamed about leaving you up on that mountain all on your lonesome. Now the spindle's here, and Squarmy's all dithered up."

"Ah . . ." William nodded as he turned and looked at his mother. *Ma touched it, and without the green stone it didn't kill her—it put her to sleep.* And then, he wondered . . .

What would happen if he could get Tuli's green stone back on the spindle? Would it replenish Morga's original thirteen deaths? Squarmy, he was sure, would be set against it.

But he had to get a full thirteen death curses on the spindle. Then they'd be rid of Morga—it was worth it, wasn't it? If he could get rid of Morga once and for all, it would make up for all the other mistakes he'd made. And she wouldn't be able to hurt anyone again.

He took a deep breath and told Tuli, "We have to get Squarmy to put the stone back on the spindle."

"Wh-at! We can't! That thing could kill you, or my lady."

"We must! It's the only way for there to be thirteen deaths on it. Morga will know if there are any less. There have to be exactly thirteen—all kindled and ready to go."

Tuli's body shook as he sighed. "And what's Morga going to do with that thing once she gets it? There be twelve good fairies what could die. And that last death. Who's that for? Yourself? Your little brother? Your ma just got a sleeping curse. If you go rekindling that full curse and get yourself killed, it'll break my lady's heart if she ever wakes."

William pursed his lips. He went to the crystal bed and touched his mother's cheek. "I have to do it," he said over his shoulder. "We can get rid of Morga, and she won't hurt anyone ever again. That's worth taking a chance—isn't it?"

"Aye. But what about her daughter? Her thirteenth daughter? She could be worse than Morga!"

William slumped onto the platform by the bed. He hadn't thought of that. He raised his head and lifted his arms wide. "What else can I do? She'll take Pinch. She'll hurt him. Maybe . . ."

William rubbed his head. "Maybe I should take the full curse and not just half of it. Then the royal curse will be finished once and for all, and Pinch can inherit the throne someday. In the meantime, we could get Squarmy to hide the spindle again—in case Morga's daughter comes looking for it."

"No!" Tuli cried.

William looked into Tuli's eyes and pleaded, "I have to do something! If I finish the tasks, Morga will leave. That's part of the old riddle. She said she can't change that. And it might be safer for the good fae, too, if she's gone forever."

Tuli's lower lip was quivering as he pulled at his beard. "I don't like it, I tell you."

William rose. He looked down at his mother. The sight of her helped him get his next words out. "I don't know if she touched the spindle on . . . on purpose or if it happened by accident. But my ma was courageous, and if she was brave enough to try to stop this, I can be, too."

Then William stiffened his spine and raised his shoulders. "I *must* be. If I'm not, Morga will raise Pinch as her son. And she'll just have him do all this again, once he's old enough."

Tuli put his head in his hands. "I—I don't want to lose you. You're my friend."

"Tuli, you're my friend, too. And I wouldn't take this chance if I didn't have to. But if I don't, we'll never be free of Morga. And my mother will sleep forever. I can't live with that. I've got to try."

Tuli reached up for William's hand and held it a moment. "If something happens to you, you'll never have to worry about my lady. And I'll find little Pinch and protect him, too."

"I know you will," William said. "You're a good guardian."

chapter 41

Coaxing and promises didn't convince Squarmy to help with the plan. In the end, Tuli had to pull from his beard all sorts of small treasures that the dragon had stashed and threaten to smash the whole lot with his cudgel.

William felt sorry for his little friend as he watched Squarmy push the green stone toward the open box. The small dragon was jerking this way and that. Still, he kept his tail wrapped firmly around the gemstone, for Tuli had his club raised above his precious hoard.

With a heave, Squarmy somersaulted into the box and pulled the stone over with his tail. He wiggled it into place. And then, like a tiny bolt of lightning, the dragon jumped from the spindle straight up into Tuli's beard. The spindle was complete.

William caught his breath. The gems glowed. And the stone! Oh! It wanted him to touch it. A voice in his head told him he needed to touch it *right now!* He leaned in.

Tuli's voice seemed to come from far away. "No!"

What was that? William shook his head, but still he raised a finger. Suddenly, a loud bray startled him. *Whin-nee . . . Aw-ah-aw!* He jerked and looked through one of the archways. Lorna-Belle stood by the hedge. And the hedge . . .

William ducked under the ivy to get a better look at it and was almost blown off the step. The hedge was leaning in as though a great wind was pushing it over. William braced himself and saw that on the other side of the hedge, all was still—not a tree branch rustled. Was this Squarmy's doing? He swiveled, and the wind blew him back into the room. The box's lid had slammed shut.

"Wh-at?" William blinked. He felt as if he'd been wandering in some hazy gray place and the sun had suddenly poked through. He peeked outside; all was calm again. Then he turned to Tuli. "Was that windstorm one of Squarmy's?"

"Don't seem like it. He likes rain and lightning. Could be the hedge decided to act up, since it be put there by the fae. And it's a right good thing it did! You weren't listening to me or Lorna-Belle."

William shivered. He locked the box. Then he lightly touched Tuli's beard. "Thank you, Squarmy. I know you didn't want to replace the stone. I wish I could think of another way to do this, but I can't. And thanks for the windstorm, if that was one of yours. It saved my life."

William put the box in his pocket. When he looked up, Tuli was sitting with his spit bucket on his head. But Tuli's head was now too large for the bucket to cover it completely, so it sat atop his balding dome like a dented metal hat. William looked into his friend's blue eyes. "And thank you," he said. "Now I have to call Morga, so . . ."

Tuli said, "I—I won't be far."

William nodded and watched his friend leave. He heard thunder. Then he placed one of his hands on his mother's hands. The room had grown dark. And Lorna-Belle had moved to munch on the new leaves of the ivy in the rain.

The storm had returned. And except for when the room was lit by lightning, it was hard for William to see. He gripped his mother's hands. *"Blacker than night is death's icy kindle.* Come! I have thirteen for Morga—fixed on a spindle."

During a flash of lightning, he saw Morga. She was standing near the foot of his mother's bed in a black gown that glittered.

"Of course you'd call me during one of the storms that vile creature manages to make. Just another example of your ill manners." Morga cried out, "Squarmy, you piece of filth! Stop the storm this instant! I know you and Tuli can hear me. You're too lazy to run far."

The rain stopped and the sky cleared. Now William could see that the witch was resting her long arms on the edge of the crystal bed. She was looking at his mother. "Still sleeping. What a pity! However, if she'd returned my spindle when she had it, she might not have touched it. But such is life."

The witch sidled closer to him. "Well, have you finished your third task? I hope so, for I'd really rather not be stuck with pouty Pinch. And I do hope you're not going to do something stupid again—like your other mistakes. Or—"

William couldn't think about mistakes right now. He had to get through this quickly, or he might not have the nerve to do it at all. He cut her off. "I have your toy."

She came toward him. "Let me have it!"

He backed away. "You have to wake my mother first."

The witch stopped; her face darkened. "Haven't I told you that no one gives me orders!" But in the next moment she was smiling and shaking her head. "Silly child! I don't know how to wake your mother. I don't know anything about taking curses off. Why ever would I bother to learn that?"

William felt his heart sinking. "You said I could be reunited with my mother."

"You truly have not been listening." She laughed.

"You *are* reunited with your mother, aren't you? I mean . . ." She pointed at his mother. "Here she is, and here you are. You're together! I didn't say *how* you'd be reunited."

She clucked her tongue at him and tilted her head. "Well, what have you tried already? Did you try kissing her? I've heard that's always a good way to rid a princess of a curse. Ah! I can see by your face that a kiss didn't work. Well, you should never put faith in those old tales." She tapped her chin.

"Did you try dancing around her on a full-moon night with three boughs of holly in your left hand and three newts in your right hand? No?" She turned and walked away. "Good. Because it doesn't work. But it's always good for a laugh."

"This is not funny!" William snapped. He clenched his fists and could feel his fingernails biting into his hands.

"No," the witch said. "I suppose it's not. After all, you and your brother have been deprived of your mother all this time. And a mother is important! Believe me, I know. And just think, if not for your mother's clumsiness, your father might still be alive. I doubt Lirian touched the spindle on purpose. Your mother just wasn't that brave. And what a father! He wasn't too smart, was he? A mother who's a cowardly thief, and a father who's a simpleton, wandering around Cliven Rock. Really, the world would be a better place if we could all choose our parents, wouldn't it?"

William squeezed his eyes shut for a moment. Then he opened them wide. "He didn't go to Cliven Rock to gather the light. He went—" William stopped himself. She was doing her best to anger him. . . . *Why?*

Strangely, with that thought he felt very calm. He had what she wanted. He breathed in evenly as he eyed her. He would not let her upset him and put him off his guard. He had to do this right. No more mistakes.

Calmly, he took the box out of his pocket. He laid it on the floor.

Morga grabbed it. She clutched it to her chest. Her black gown began to writhe around her. In its dark folds William thought he could see teeth—tiny teeth that snapped as the dress whirled to life. He gripped the side of the crystal bed.

The fae witch glared at William, all pretense of concern gone. "At last!" she said. Then she chanted . . .

Whiter than snow is love's light atremble.
Thirteen for Morga—scooped in a thimble.

Redder than blood are flames that will brand.
Thirteen for Morga—clutched in bare hand.

Blacker than night is death's icy kindle.
Thirteen for Morga—fixed on a spindle.

A thimble of love.
A handful of flame.
A spindle of death—

"And you'll go whence you came," William finished for her, adding, "My tasks are done. You promised to never go near Pinch if I helped you get your toy. And you said you'd go away."

"Don't worry about your precious Pinch," she said. "I don't need him now. Besides, human children are disgusting, always slobbering. Mind you, he did get better, didn't he? So don't think yourself high and mighty! I've fulfilled my part of our agreement. A fae doesn't fail to fulfill a true pact. And you've gained something, as well. You've learned to listen better before entering into a bargain."

William could hear Morga fumbling with the box as she spoke. A moment later, she demanded, "Where's the key?"

"It's hidden."

"Hidden!" she shrieked. "Find it now! Or I'll unleash my pets."

And William saw that the teeth sprinkled throughout her gown belonged to grimwyrms.

chapter 42

The witch bounded toward William, her hands so close to his face that he could feel the heat of her skin. But she did not touch him.

"I don't have the key on me," William said. "And if you harm me, you'll never find it."

Morga whirled. The teeth in her black gown snapped at him. "Your tasks are *not* done!"

He took another breath to steady himself. "Yes, they are. I delivered the spindle with thirteen deaths on it. You did not say *how* I needed to deliver it. And so I brought the deaths to you in a locked box."

"No!" screamed Morga. "No! No! No!"

She tried to pry open the lid. "All my pretty deaths! I need you."

William reached down and took his mother's hands in his. "I will give you the key when you wake my mother."

"She's got it, hasn't she?" Morga rushed to his mother's side and bent toward her. Then she yanked her hands back, not wanting to touch his mother. "Get it for me, or my pets will feast on you!"

"No." William shook his head. "Instead, I propose a new pact."

"What?"

The witch was so close, her rank breath clouded William's thoughts for a moment. *Had he gotten this right?* His voice came out shaky. "You—you want the spindle for your thirteenth daughter's feast day, don't you? And I want my mother awakened. It's a simple pact. I will take the key from my mother and give it to you, *after* you wake her up . . . today."

Morga stomped off the platform and across the floor. Abruptly, she turned back to him and smiled. "It's a solemn pact! I agree."

"Agreed," William said. "A solemn pact."

The fae witch rubbed her chin. "This may take a moment. As I said, I did not always keep up on how to undo curses. Oh, yes! *Now* I remember. It's simple. The only way she'll awaken is when another royal heir takes her place! You, perhaps?" And now the witch's black tongue came out to lick her teeth.

William nodded and took a shaky breath. "Agreed."

Morga's eyes widened. "Aren't we brave!" She gave a hiss. "Very well, I agree, too! It's a pact. Now—"

"Tuli!" William called, interrupting her.

Tuli appeared at the other side of the crystal bed. His cudgel hung from his belt.

Morga put her hands on her hips. "Well! If it isn't Tuli, the would-be guardian. And a decent size today. Whatever you do, don't let that slippery piece of filth that lives in your beard out. The sight of those things sickens me—there's no telling what I might do!"

Tuli was pale, and his hands shook. He did not raise his eyes to meet Morga's.

Morga smiled. "Just think. Soon your beautiful lady will walk away, and all you'll have is a dirt-streaked boy to watch over. Surely you'll be able to manage that without messing up."

Morga put her hands on her hips. "Well, we're all here but Moggety. Where is she? Isn't this some sort of farewell party for you? Actually, I quite like the idea. All those tears I'll get to see when you take your mother's place."

William reached into his shirt and grasped Moggety's vial. A green haze floated into the room, and in the center of it was Moggety. Her arms were folded, and she had a stern look on her face.

Morga clapped her hands. "I see you're getting a little better at your sendings. Too bad you haven't been able to figure out how to keep mine away from your hearth, eh?" Then she took a turn along the end of the crystal bed, where she threw a hand into the air and laughed. "If you think you're intimidating me with such a ragtag crowd, you're greatly mistaken." Suddenly, she leaned over the glass bed and snarled at William, "I don't have any more time to waste. We have a pact. And since everyone's here to give you some courage, you will take your mother's place. Now!"

William nodded. "I will."

Tuli leaned over the bed and lifted out his lady.

"What's going on?" the fae witch asked, looking from William to Tuli.

"I'm taking her place," William said as he climbed onto the glass bed. "Then she'll awaken. You gave your word in a solemn pact. After that, I'll hand you the key."

Morga's mouth dropped open as Moggety laughed.

The witch grabbed at her hair. "No!" she screamed. "You have to be in a deep sleep to take her place."

"I *was* listening," William said. "Tuli and Moggety are my witnesses. They heard the oath. Falling into a sleep was not part of our pact. I only had to take her place. And I have."

On the bed, William folded his hands on his chest, still clasping Moggety's vial. He waited. Tuli stood close with his lady cradled against his chest.

"No!" The witch stretched her arms into the air. "You have to sleep first!"

Now William smiled. "How can I, if I'm the one to hand you the key? Weren't you listening?"

Morga crumpled. She banged her fists against the stone floor.

William said, "If you want your heirloom, wake her now."

"You must abide by your solemn oath," Moggety said, pointing a finger at the witch. "You know what will happen if you do not. The hedge can hear us; your sisters will know if you do not keep your vow."

Slowly, Morga rose to her feet. Her eyes were fiery. Her mouth was a purple smear in her contorted face. She rounded the bed toward Tuli and William's mother.

Tuli started to back away.

"Stand still, you lump!" Morga stretched out one bony finger and lightly touched each of William's mother's eyes. The witch groaned and clutched at her hand as though she'd been seared. Then she buried her hand in the endless dark of her gown. Her leathery face was twisted with pain.

William saw his mother's eyelids twitch. They opened. They closed again. And then one slender hand rose, and she covered her mouth as she yawned. His mother was awake!

William sat up. "Ma!" He let the vial drop against his chest as he clambered over the side of the bed. Tuli set her gently on her feet and she swayed. William caught her.

"My key!" Morga screamed. "Now!'

William took the key from where his mother clutched

261

it in one hand. He held it out by his fingertips. Morga carefully snatched it.

"Wha-what's going on?" his mother asked. She yawned again.

"What's going on?" cried Morga, frantically unlocking the box. "This!" she shrieked, and yanked the spindle free.

Morga lunged at William with the spindle held high. "And now, you'll die!"

William looked up just as a yellow blur leapt from Tuli's beard. It landed on the spindle, and a green jewel flipped up and flew through the air.

Morga stabbed downward. William was ready to take his mother's place.

But in the same instant, a loud *Whinnee . . . Aw-ah-aw!* filled the room. A dark shape blocked the light, and a hard hoof kicked the witch.

Morga sprawled, sliding off the platform. The spindle, free of her grasp, landed by Tuli. It went spinning around and around like a toy.

"Ahh!" William's mother cried.

That was the moment when Tuli slammed his cudgel down on the crystal spindle, shattering it and its bone whorl and scattering all its blood-red rubies. Then he did it once more—just in case he'd messed up the first time.

chapter 43

Morga dragged herself upright. She slapped Lorna-Belle aside and staggered out. And William thought he heard the witch cry, "All lost, my precious daughter! All lost!"

"Did you see that?" Tuli crowed. "I did it with my ma's cudgel." He patted his club.

William had gone limp. But he managed to make his legs hold him up. Then he smiled at Tuli and helped to steady his mother, who stood with her mouth open— speechless and blinking in the light.

William thought the smashed spindle was free of the deaths it had held. Still, Squarmy carefully pushed all its broken pieces into its box. Then he tucked the green stone into the curve of his tail.

William locked the box again.

His mother leaned against her bed. When she had composed herself, she said, "We'll hide the pieces some-place beyond the reach of any fae witch. Just in case." Then she touched Tuli's hand. "To my brave guardian, I pledge my unending love and gratitude for a job well done."

Tuli turned bright purple. He groped about for his spit bucket and balanced it on top of his large head.

William's mother laughed.

She laughed! And the sound, like tiny bells, made William's heart dance. Oh, how he had wanted to hear that sound again! He put his arms around her middle and squeezed. "Ma!"

She put a hand on William's shoulder. "Take care of your friend's needs first. Then we'll talk. I think that—that mule needs attending to."

William whipped around and looked at Lorna-Belle, who was frantically trying to lick her flank. "What's happened?" he asked. Pushing her head to one side, he saw a handprint branded onto her rump. Morga had left her mark. "Come! Let's get you up to the spring on the ridge. We'll cool it off."

As William led Lorna-Belle out, he saw that the clearing had changed. Except for a very small section, the hedge was gone. He turned in a slow circle. *What?*

Lorna-Belle whinnied.

"I'll figure this out later," he told her.

At the spring he filled his hands with water and poured it over Lorna-Belle's burn. He stroked her neck. "I don't know, Lorna-Belle. Somehow, I think you're more than just a plain old mule! Thank you." And before he left her to rest in the shade, he kissed her on the end of her freckled muzzle. "From now on, you can slobber on me all you want."

Back inside the building, Tuli was beaming. The spit bucket was off his head.

William's mother smiled, too. "Tell me all that's happened. I don't even know how long I've slept. But I do remember visitors who brightened my heart. I know your father has been here."

"About Da . . . ," William began, and faltered as the tears fell.

It was a sad telling, and they clung to each other afterward. Later, his mother dried her eyes and said, "It's time to go home. There's Pinch to attend to, and I want to visit your father's grave." She turned to Tuli. "Will you come as well?"

Tuli had cried as he heard William tell of his father's death. But he had kept crying into a rag long after William had finished talking. Now he tugged at his red beard and looked up at William and his mother, blubbering. "Squarmy's gone!"

"Gone?" William looked around. "Where?"

"He's just . . . gone!" Tuli wailed. "My friend! He took Da's stone and shoved off. I'll not see the likes of such a fine fellow again. *Waaaah!* He was the best, the most upstandingest, honest body anyone could know!"

Lirian knelt by Tuli's side. She patted his shoulder.

"I don't understand," said William. "Isn't he somewhere nearby?"

Tuli shook his head but couldn't speak. "He's . . . *Waaaaah!*"

"I think I understand," said William's mother. "It was the job of the dragons to protect the members of the royal family from Morga. But if she is no more, then . . ."

"Then there are no more dragons!" William cut in,

putting his hand to his head. "But Morga's not dead! We didn't kill her." William rushed out. Maybe . . .

He glanced at the bit of hedge remaining. *That's odd.* This short section was bright green. And William could swear it sat where the gap used to be. He went to inspect it and jumped back with his hand over his mouth. Pushing the thick new foliage aside, he'd found Morga—or rather, what was left of her. The hedge had crushed her, and a thorn had pierced her heart.

For a moment, he wondered why the hedge hadn't killed her before. And then he knew: the good fae had waited. *Yes.* They'd waited until the spindle was destroyed and they were safe. He had helped the fae. He nodded to himself. *Yes.* And they'd made Morga go away for good—just as the riddle had said.

But now . . . the dragons were gone, too.

William fell to his knees. He hadn't said good-bye to Squarmy. His tears watered the grass in the glade. This time, he wept for his friend Squarmy. For Tuli. And for Pinch, who would never meet a real dragon.

chapter 44

Tuli stayed on in the old Forest. And until the end of his days, he would keep a constant eye out for a tiny dragon. It was not difficult for him to do, either. For when the friends awakened the next morning, the hedge was completely gone, and Tuli was a giant! He barely fit in the glade. His cudgel looked like a toothpick, and his spit bucket fit his finger as a thimble.

William and his mother were careful as they climbed up on his knee to say good-bye.

Tuli was careful not to swoosh them away with his booming words and his heaving river of salty tears.

Later, Lorna-Belle, William and his mother headed home. On their way, they stopped at the burying ground, where William and his mother placed wildflowers on Da's grave.

His mother said, "I must go soon to see my father, the king."

"The king!" William kept forgetting that his mother was a princess. "Moggety said he's my grandfather."

She touched his cheek. "Yes, he is. You look like him."

"I do?"

She nodded. "Especially your eyes. And it's been a long while since he's seen you. He'll be overjoyed to hear that Morga is no more."

"Will we go back up to our house at the peak?"

"Oh, yes," she said. "I'm not ready to become a *real* princess yet. And I want to feel your da around me again. It's on the crag we were the happiest. Also, I need to get out of this gown and into something comfortable. Ha!"

She rose slowly from the graveside. "One day, when

your grandfather needs me, we will have to live in a stuffy old castle with servants and down beds. Will you mind? No more howling winds and freezing cold?"

William rolled his eyes. "I won't mind, so long as there's more food than turnips and apples at the castle."

His mother laughed. "I'm sure there is."

Then she bit her lip and in a quiet voice said, "William, I am terribly sorry. I—I made such a mess of everything!"

"What do you mean? I'm the one that made a mess of things! I invited Morga into the house when I knew better. I'm sorry, Ma."

"No, William. The fault lies not with you. There is still much to sort out. But it was that spindle!" His mother looked off across all the gravestones and crosses. "It has called to me my whole life, as I'm sure it had to many of my ancestors. But I was the weak one. I—"

William interrupted her. "You weren't weak! You were brave and strong."

She shrugged. "Was I? Perhaps I was simply being willful. I thought if I could find it, I could destroy it, or . . . or somehow change it so it wouldn't harm you and Pinch." She trailed off and was quiet for a few moments. "I was just tired of the curse hounding our family. And I knew Morga would find us, sooner or later, up on the mountain.

"About a year ago, the Dightby flooded. And I knew

something that had lain hidden had moved. I followed that call and came to the Old Forest. I found the box snagged by an ancient willow. The tree was split at its heart and its rotted roots lifted. And there it sat, entwined in the dying willow's grasp. I knew what it was right away. The thing was evil, even locked in its box." His mother paused for a moment and brushed her hair from her face. "I didn't do anything for a day or so—and I did not have the key, anyway. I sat there thinking. And then a strange thing happened."

"What?"

"As I sat on a rock by the river, a crow flew by and dropped something shiny into the shallows. I thought it might have dropped a small fish. But it was a key. I wasn't surprised. Crows like to collect bright things. Then, when I found that it fit into the lock on the box, it all felt right. I knew I had to open the box."

She bent a little and looked into William's face. "You've seen the spindle. You know how it pulls at the royal blood in you. That was part of Morga's curse—that it would draw us to it."

He nodded. "It wanted me to touch it, especially after the green stone was put back on."

"Yes," his mother whispered. She resettled the jeweled circlet on her head. "I'm so glad you didn't! Well, I don't know, exactly, what happened after I opened the box. I don't know if I touched it, thinking I would take on the curse and free my children. But I do know that thought was in my mind. Be that as it may, I remember closing my eyes and falling. Afterward, sometimes, there were people nearby who loved me. I could sense that. And I was sad—so incredibly sad."

"Your tears were golden, and they lit up the whole glade."

"Were they? I didn't know I could cry golden tears."

"And silver-white ones, too. They helped me with Morga's first task."

His mother dabbed at her eyes. "You say Heldor fell from Cliven Rock when he hid the box up there?"

"Yes."

"He must have found the spindle by my side. It wouldn't have hurt him. He has no royal blood. And he knew all about the curse; I told him before we were married." She thought for a moment, and added, "You said Morga claimed he was working on the finding spell?"

"Yes. She said Da had made a pact with her." William paused. "But how could he have, unless . . ."

"Yes," said his mother. "Unless she approached him after he'd found me, but before he'd gotten up to Cliven Rock. Oh!" She put her hand on her heart. "Your father was very brave! It's a good thing she didn't know he had it with him."

Her eyes were big as William nodded at her. Then

they looked at Da's simple grave marker. "Can we put up a nicer memorial for him?" William asked.

"We will certainly do that." She gathered him in her arms. "We'll have a beautiful memorial made for him. I'll sell this silly crown I'm wearing to pay for it."

At Moggety's cottage, Pinch leapt up at his mother before she could even slide off Lorna-Belle. "Mama! Mama!"

Slipping off the mule, his mother twirled down the path. Her copper-colored hair floated about her as she held Pinch in her arms. "How's my little man?" she cried. "I've dreamed of you so often!"

Moggety clapped her hands. Staring at Lirian and Pinch, she exclaimed, "Now, that's a grand sight! And I'll wager we'll have a grand story to hear tonight. That is, I would if I was a wagering woman. Hah!" She went off into peals of laughter.

Then Pinch, slipping from his mother, ran around everyone's legs, snatching up the kittens. "Look, Mama! Moggety let me name them. This one's Lirian. See the color of her fur? And this one's Heldor, after Da." He showed her the gray one. "Only—" Pinch stumbled on the words, his lips trembling. "Only, Da's dead. That's what William says."

His mother knelt by him. "I know." She stroked the gray cat. "Those are fine names you gave them. I'm pleased. Also, I was wondering how you'd like to have your father's name now. He was a good man, and it's a good name. Heldor."

"Heldor?" Pinch threw his arms out. "Yes!" And then he ran to William, and to Moggety, crying, "I'm Heldor. That's my real name! My really true big-person name. Just like Da!"

William laughed.

Lorna-Belle shook her head. *Whinnee . . . Aw-ah-aw!*

William turned to Moggety and lifted the chain and vial over his head. "Thank you," he said, handing them back to her.

Moggety smiled and planted a kiss on William's head. "Love is powerful," she said. Then she slipped the chain on, and the blue vial glowed as it lay in its rightful place, next to her heart.

That night, William's mother and Moggety sat in a deep whispering conversation. William saw his mother unwrap the spindle's box and hand it to Moggety. He wondered where she would hide it. But he didn't have a lot of time to worry about that, for Pinch had jumped out from behind the curtain wall and landed on him.

The kittens, too, tumbled. When no one was looking, Heldor scooted a stolen wooden thimble into his secret hoard behind the bench. And Lirian twitched her ears before she pounced on him. Her orange fur, on end, looked like flames.

Epilogue

It is good, hardworking folk who tell stories by firesides, while traveling long roads, or to settle cranky babies. It is a way of remembering.

Oh, yes.

One of the best tales is about a young hero, a haeftling dragon and a blue-eyed giant—a Yana.

Oh, yes.

There were giants in those days, and dragons.

And in those days an ancient evil was destroyed— its remains dropped into the fiery heart of an old forest.

Now, when this story is told, all agree that it ends as stories should.

The good folk in it lived . . . happily ever after.

Acknowledgments

William and the Witch's Riddle came about because of my love for folktales and fairy tales. Through the heart of these stories—despite magical trappings and fantastical events—flows human desire. There are the dark downward pulls of jealousy, hate and corrupting power, as well as the joyful upwellings of love, justice and sudden good luck. Why not extend these tales—retell them by infusing them with a bit of my own imagination? Why not, especially when a wonderful editor like Michelle Frey is constantly challenging me?

In addition to Michelle Frey at Alfred A. Knopf and the great folks who work with her, I owe heartfelt thanks to two insightful critique groups: my Michigan group, made up of Valerie Carey, Cecily Donnelly, Tracy Gallup, Debbie Gonzales, Mary Lind, Deb Pilutti, Ginny Ryan, Nancy Shaw, Debbie Taylor, Shanda Trent, Hope Vestergaard and Liza Wheeler; and my Florida group, made up of Audrey Ades, Sylvia Andrews, Ruth Darrington, Laura

Fournier, Donna Gephart, Lori Houran, Linda Marlow, Jill Nadler, Becca Puglisi, Stacie Ramey, Dan Rousseau and Gail Shepherd. Also, I owe more thanks to two librarian beta readers whose expertise I could not do without, Paula Schaffner and Sherry Roberts—both connoisseurs of folk literature and fantasy. Finally, I must acknowledge my husband and family, who put up with me while I'm in the throes of creating. They understand why I occasionally appear to be addle-tweaked!